Cleaning House

CLEANING HOUSE

NANCY HAYFIELD

Farrar · Straus · Giroux

NEW YORK

For My Mother

 / First printing, 1980
Printed in the United States of America
Published simultaneously in Canada by
McGraw-Hill Ryerson Ltd., Toronto
Designed by Cynthia Krupat
Second printing, 1981
Library of Congress Cataloging in Publication Data
Hayfield, Nancy. / Cleaning house.
I. Title.
PZ4. H41865Cl [PS3558.A839] 813'.54 80-19029

Cleaning House

Consider the thin, crackly, wrapping paper skin of the onion, as I did this morning while cleaning out the refrigerator. It's like any explanation I can offer him—totally superfluous. He'll only hear that word, way down the end of any sentence. Orgy.

"What?"

"Orgy."

"Where?"

"Here."

"*Here*—in my own house?"

In your own house, and bed, and living room, and wife, and kitchen . . .

I begin each time with why, with fragile excuses covering more fragile excuses like umber onion skin: transparent, flaking loose under pressure . . .

"Why?"

Why clean out the refrigerator?

It was a long chain of events, to be sure. First, there was the heat, the incredible, globed Indian-summer air that pressed up to my face and settled down on top of my body like a confident lover, forcing itself into my brain with warm gloved fingers, pressing away my dreams, layer by layer, until I was close to morning, nearly awake. I could hear someone shuffling down the hall and the cars going swish, swish, back and forth, in the dark inky rain. When I opened my eyes there was no rain, only stabbing Dracula-bright sun, and the sound of Toby opening the refrigerator and clinking bottles and glasses in the kitchen, trying to find something to drink. When I turned to see what time it was, I felt my head splinter with a starburst of pain, and I closed my eyes and held still so I would stay in one piece on the pillow. My head was a mosaic, a broken eggshell, held by an invisible membrane that you shouldn't press too hard—like Maggie's windshield after the rock hit it last night.

I tried to climb back into the dream, but it was as futile as trying to fit back into my wedding gown, so I pulled the crazy quilt up around my legs and drifted on the edge of things for another ten minutes. Then there was a loud crash from the kitchen as I stepped off a deep dream curb and fell back into the bed, ripping the quilt with my big toenail, which I had grown and polished especially for the orgy. I pulled the quilt off my foot and the roily memories from last night came crowding in. Hairy, naked thighs were slapping against vanilla-pudding thighs, and then there was a new swishing sound from the kitchen, so I had to leave the thighs rubbing under the quilt and go feed and clean this gaping mouth of a morning before I could get back to reconstructing the orgy.

Thank God for a job! I could hear Toby beginning to cry now because he had scared himself with the crash, and it's easy, once you're needed, to lower your horizon until you're in a long, low tunnel which you simply scrub through to the end, keeping your mind only on the job at hand. That way, I could walk past the wrecked living room without looking in, move smoothly past it all and not touch it. It looked as if a movie set had been struck in there, so much equipment and fantasy were waiting and still. Angular piles of dirty glasses, game pieces, napkin puffs, and fallen pillows all crawled toward the doorway at me, and I knew I could ignore it for a little while longer if I cleaned something else instead.

Toby had tried to pour a leftover quart of whiskey sours over the mouth of a shot glass he had found on the kitchen counter. When the glass tipped over in the streaming yellow waterfall, he hid it in the refrigerator, where he knocked over the orange juice that had been pushed behind all the leftover bottles of beer on the shelf. And now he was crying, screaming, and the first thing I had to do was to stop the noise throbbing against the weak glass of my eyes, so I unwrapped a triangle of Laughing Cow cheese that someone had stuck in the telephone book and wedged it into his mouth. He clamped down on it, surprised, and smiled around its wet edges as I lifted him into his high chair.

My bare feet sucked off the sticky linoleum each time I walked back to the sink to rinse the orange-juice-soaked rag in clear water, and I began to enjoy the big mess once I saw its dimensions completely. Standing in the middle of it made it less scary than it had sounded from the bedroom, more like a Truth or Consequences game show stunt once I was here in the kitchen. The sun glinted off a lake of orange juice that puddled under the shot glass on the cutting board and dribbled slowly over the front of the counter, drop by drop, into the silverware drawer.

"Who did you sleep with?"

Under the counter it ran, a bloated yellow tributary snaking across my green embossed floor . . .

"With more than one guy?"

It was all over the front of the stove, freckled in little round bumps on the legs of the telephone table, souring the water in the cat's dish. It even splashed up the dress of one of Maggie's angels.

"Two at the same time?"

Now, stickiness, like grease, is invisible, after the fact. You must clean by touch, rather than by sight . . .

"Where, where did you do it?"

Wipe, and touch for tacky, slimy, gritty, or slick—it's quite a mess, getting even stickier in the heat—you can feel it even if you can't see it. What's worse, it's also all over the inside of the refrigerator, all over the food, in the plate of ham, filmed over the two raw chickens, in the vegetable bins . . .

"Why?"

Finally, he would have to ask why.

Which brings me to the onions, swimming in a yellow pool of cold orange juice in the bottom of the refrigerator: Carmen Miranda onions, rolling back and forth against the rotting apples and bananas in this cold metal bin. We're having a heat wave, a tropical heat wave. And the deep banana fragrance flitters up in waves off the metal sides of the big airplane that ticks in the Puerto Rican sun, and now the honeymoon is finally over. Toby castanets his spoon against the metal tray of his high chair, and life could be so beautiful if I hadn't done this terrible thing last night. Sweet innocent baby! Poor innocent husband, flying home to me right this very minute, as unaware of any orgy as he's unaware of the dark swarmy cities crawling below the gentle cloud cover out his airplane window. He's still innocent, cradled up there in the heavens, and now I'm not—I'm down here among all the broken pieces of our marriage contract. This is the worst thing I've ever done, and I don't even believe in confession any more.

So, I'll clean the refrigerator, my alter ego, instead. God knows, I felt more violated when the person from Michigan that Maggie invited pushed his six-pack of Michelob onto my clean milk shelf than when he later pushed his . . .

Ah, ah, ah—no dirty thoughts! No dirty thoughts—I'm cleaning the refrigerator. The problem is that when you've just had an experience, details play and replay in your mind, fresh and unobstructed, whether you want them to or not. They gambol about and linger like little children, pressing up close to you, innocent of any moral tags, until you consciously get up there and discriminate, push some aside, hide a few, and keep the others. And besides, I'll wear out all the good ones if I allow them casual access. I figure each scene has one gut-wrenching, stomach-strumming pang of recognition, and then two or three warm washes of wallowing before it becomes stale, used up, unable to excite me any more. The best part of all this is the fakir's basket of snakes I've now got stored away in my memory, just waiting to be summoned up, up; to writhe back and forth in my brain like these wilted carrots curling over the old tan cauliflower here in the vegetable bin.

It's all here in the vegetable bin, the secret of life. All I have to do is to find the little devil. "Is it you, you slimy celery? Come up here out of the orange juice and talk to me—tell me what I should do about this mess." But the rotting tops shrink and flatten, cling back against my hand: the green seaweed fingers are taciturn and lifeless, secreting no watery answers.

This job is endless, because my refrigerator, like my brain, is stuffed with garbage. I've got ideas from Maggie going stale next to failed, uneaten casseroles. Useless tidbits from the *Ladies' Home Journal* are stuffed in the corners with the baking soda, and untouched remains of memories from Aunt Ruth are rotting in their sealed containers. I am past the point of opening some of them and I can see through the sides that the stuff in there is now frosted over with green mold, fuzzy on the top, slimy like an oyster on the bottom. If you want to know someone, just open her refrigerator, and there's her personality, all spread out. I know I'm right: the real person is in there with the telltale chewed cheese, the optimistic yogurt, or the squishy lazy cap on the bottle of catsup. If someone cared enough to examine your refrigerator, she'd know what you know about yourself. After all, it's true what the Salada tea bags say: "You are what you are only when no one is looking."

Well, my refrigerator is always full because I grew up poor and I've always hated to cook, so I'm afraid to throw things away or to be without a great supply of food for emergencies. The two chickens I bought a week ago for tonight's dinner are still in there, tightly wrapped in Saran, crowded together in naked intimacy on their plastic tray, already going bad in the heat. I was planning to cook them as a special welcome-home dinner for Jack, who says he makes enough money for me to stay home and raise our two children properly.

I hate that word, "properly." Also, "promptly," and "prepare," and "moisten." I hate being told what to do, even by printed directions, especially by recipes. And I hate to cook chicken because of the jelly goo that coagulates under it on the dish when it cools. Once I cooked a chicken neck because I felt guilty for throwing so many of them away, and when I broke it up for the skimpy pieces of meat on it, I found a boiled white worm inside. The poor chicken was killed before he even swallowed his last meal. And I hate the veins on chicken—rubber bands on the drumstick that look like little *o*'s after you bite into them. I hate to cook it, I hate to eat it—I hate this suspense, this constant waiting for Jack to come home.

But I can still do something nice with this dinner in spite of the orange juice. I just have to wash the chickens off to get rid of the slimy feeling and that slightly sweet or slightly sour odor that spreads off them when I peel the plastic film and separate their legs, their thighs, their breasts from one another. You have to quiet a lot of sensible squeamishness before you can cook or have sex. I dread sticking my fingers deep into them under the running water, but you have to feel for the organs, the little paper package with a tiny play heart, the sore-looking little kidneys and liver, and the thing that must be part of the neck that gave us Sylvia Plath's most famous simile, the one about the first time she saw her boyfriend's penis and thought it looked like a turkey neck. Of course, my aunt always cooked these things in a small pot of water, leaving the most desperate scum for me to scrub away from the sides of the pot—a miniature bathtub ring made of rubber cement. So I always throw the little bag out unopened.

However, to throw the bloody organs away does not necessarily mean I will be done with them. No, my aunt will be picking blackly through my garbage later, making small clucking noises, telling me I waste too much, I will burn in Purgatory for the clean pieces of paper I throw away, kill off a few starving babies in China for the food, and send us all to the poorhouse one day for using Saran Wrap, ScotTowels, and, God help us, Handi-Wipes. Disposables! The cheap and quiet servants of poor people—they could be the symbol of my liberation, according to Maggie, who lives down the street.

"Go out and buy the stupid stuff, live with it, get used to the convenience—and the guilt will go away when you throw it all out with the garbage," she said, the last time she was packing. And as I carried home a box of her stuff to store in my hall closet, she shouted after me, "You'll wonder how you ever lived without paper towels in the house!"

Now, my aunt never throws anything away. You remember the one kid who brought her lunch to school in a Sunbeam bread bag? It was me. I never had a paper napkin the whole time I went to school. I eat very neatly, still. Maggie told me I should go out and buy some fabric softener, air freshener, Brillo pads, and individual packages of Cup-a-Soup at the store. But my aunt muttered and moaned all the way through the market, held me by the coat sleeve, and repeated her litany of money-saving household hints: "You take the clothes right off the line and shake them out, hard, then you won't need no fabric softener. Don't use so much soap, they won't be so stiff, don't leave them on the line overnight—then they'll smell good. Open the windows if you want fresh air. What are you, crazy? Buying a can of *air*? Soak the dirty pans overnight, use a little elbow grease and nylon net, and here—soup bones are cheap, ends of vegetables are cheap, how do you think we made ends meet? Don't throw nothing out—don't be such a spendthrift—one of these days you'll be hungry. You'll be looking through your own garbage for what you need. Who do you think you are, anyway?"

Or something to that effect. And I have to admit that I do wish I had the courage to roll the shopping cart over her ripped and mended black shoe just to stop the words, but of course I can't, because the poor old woman is dead. She's been dead for over a year, probably turned to ashes in the grave by now, the closest she's ever been to dirt. There is a gritty thumbprint of her on the inside of my forehead to remind me how I am permanently connected to her and to the Lenten dust forever under my bed. So I hear her talking all the time, even though she is out of place in a neighborhood as fancy as this one is. "You're on the bed for a few years, and then you're the dust, and under it forever," she used to say, pushing a clicking dust mop ahead of her on the linoleum, making it come alive at the corners of the room, wriggling over the baseboards, sniffing under the radiators. Her ashes have more potency now than fancy Colombian espresso to spring to bitter dark life, wherever and whenever she wants, staining the present.

"Who do you think you are?" Maggie recently asked me in a playful tone, while crossing her legs and dangling one sandaled foot over the Persian carpet in her kitchen. I watched her painted toes peep like graded cherries from under the leather lattice of her sandal, and of course, I thought of Aunt Ruth's big black thumbnail, dead from a factory accident before I ever knew her. The industrial sewing machine needle had stitched right through her thumb, and she even had to put the machine into reverse and turn one more stitch back into her thumb to free her finger before she could get to the nurse's station. The nurse told her she was really lucky not to have lost the whole thumb, considering. My aunt said she watched the fingernail blacken and die, but still stay on her thumb, held by the white thread that had dried to a deep purple-red from her blood.

I once told Maggie that I could answer the question "*What* are you?" but not "*Who* are you?" I think this is pretty interesting.

"So what?" she asked.

"A wife, a mother, an orphan."

"An orphan! That's so romantic! Who were your real parents?"

"Aunt Ruth's second-youngest sister and no one knows who."

"What happened to them?"

"Car accident."

"Neat! Let's try it again: What?"

"An ingrate, a frigid wife."

"That's no good. Try this: How do you *see* yourself?"

I had to think for a while. Too long, actually, for Maggie, who left without finishing her tea. But I see myself as a Modigliani head in the refrigerator handle, a chrome exclamation point. I read somewhere that Johnny Carson's second wife had her wedding ring melted down into the shape of a hard teardrop so she would remember her marriage, and Aunt Ruth used to say, "All you ever do is read." Maggie says I don't have enough experiences in life to really enjoy myself, and Jack says the purpose of life is in accepting responsibility, not in enjoyment. Who's to say who's right?

So when I'm in doubt, I always wash the dishes—it is a job

I can do quite well, and it always seems to set things right again. The house settles down when Mother washes the dishes, because once the water starts running, everyone knows where she'll be for an hour or so; taking care of things, making it pretty in the kitchen again, allowing the next day to come cleanly and unencumbered. The orgy can be gone! What power we women have—setting the world to rights again . . . and it feels so good, too . . . my wrists in cold rinse water on this sticky hot day, the refrigerator nearly clean except for the vegetable bin, Jack flying home—except for the orgy. Merely by cleaning up a mess, mistakes can be thrown out, washed away, forgotten. Salada says, "The person who never makes a mistake must get pretty tired of doing nothing," and I agree with this thought today. I mean, how was I to know if I really am frigid or not unless I put it to the ultimate test of a drunken orgy: anonymous, dark, with all my fantasies laid end to end? I rationalize: The refrigerator looks clean if you don't open the bottom drawer, and I look clean if I don't open my mouth.

But we all know it's dirty, don't we, Aunt Ruth? Maggie keeps telling me to uncover my feelings, to clean up and dig out and to bring to the surface, and I will, I will, I will tell him. I'll tell him everything! Details—the truth! I hate all these lies! And I'll throw all these rotting vegetables away, upend the vegetable bin into the sink, and wash it out once and for all.

Which is what I did for the rest of the morning. The job took longer than expected because those frivolous, skimpy onion skins, which I thought superfluous, proved instead to be indomitable, glued by the orange juice in fibrous stripes and crisscrosses all over the metal bottom of the bin, speaking to me in stubborn, squeaky, vegetable hieroglyphics.

Because I was lonely?

Because I wanted to see if I really was frigid?

Because I wanted a disposable experience?

Because I really am black and spoiled rotten on the inside?

Or maybe all of the above?

It all began when I met Maggie a year ago.

"I'm an artist," she said, again and again. "Let me show you what I mean." Even when she's down the street, I hear her words from shady quiet corners of my house, where I've put some of the things she's made for me. Her artifacts cling to my tables and bureaus like old locust shells in the last summer sun—mute, brittle memories of something once alive but just now gone.

There is the clay pot she threw too fast and then watched as the pulling circular motion stretched it into a wavy, wobbly, misshapen egg.

"The center didn't hold," she said, with obvious joy, when she gave it to me.

The pot is colored a deep reddish tint, and if you hold it directly in the sunlight, the way Maggie showed me, and then spin it, the glaze will send little red fireflies shining off the walls, dancing a drunken voodoo spin of fire licks across the furniture and past my face in the mirror. For a minute, it looks as if Maggie herself is here in the room, dancing with the magic lantern show, harmlessly decorating the room for me, until I pull the pot from the sunlight and she disappears with the red lights.

"She's very flighty," the neighbors say.

"But I'm an artist," she would answer, as she did when she sketched each of our neighbors in quick satiric strokes one afternoon on her thick watercolor pad. She ripped off the drawings as soon as she finished each one and threw it in the fireplace. Then the neighbor who had been momentarily misjudged by her pencil would flutter softly above the choppy fire for a long minute before she would brown on the edges and burst into flame. I saved myself by reaching into the flame just as the edges of the page were curling around and back on my long apron strings. I saw something in the picture come alive for a second, and I forgot the fire and reached in to pull it out. It was a sketch of how she had pictured me before we became friends.

"Get rid of it—you're not like that any more," she said, grabbing it back. "I'll show you what you're like now."

She threw it back into the fire, stared at me for a minute, and then turned to a clean page. Her pencil began to whisper to the pad, and I fanned my scorched knees and blew on my burned finger to cool it while I waited for my newer self to emerge. My old caricatured face, now back in the fire, shuddered and drifted and began to tip into the smoldering flames, and I remembered the first time I ever wore the plaid babushka that she had sketched me wearing.

It was the day I first saw the neighborhood unrolling like a green game board in front of the tinted car windshield. The real-estate agent was narrating, and her words were as colorful and teasing as her long scarf, which was waving out the open window. "Now, here is one of our prettiest neighborhoods . . . it has the best schools . . . the country club . . . within jogging distance to the trains . . . nothing at the moment in your price range here, but I knew you'd like to see it, anyway . . . you look like such a perfect person for a house here: why don't you tell your husband to come have a look? It's a real storybook town, don't you think?"

And then abruptly we turned a corner and were back on the main road again, back to the apartments, but the agent knew —she could smell the blood lust, the animal heat, that the idea of living in that other, older, better neighborhood had stirred in me. I wanted to live there in the same desperate way I had wanted to live in the Christmas village in Aunt Ruth's train set, where tiny gray geese swam on a pocket mirror in a sea of salt. Where people never wanted to be anywhere else.

Jack was flattered because the agent said I was attractive, but realistic when I told him about the prices in the neighborhood after dinner that evening. He took out his ledger book and opened it up on the kitchen table, calculated the hours of overtime he'd need for a bigger down payment, and then turned back the lead in his gold mechanical pencil before speaking.

"I don't think we can afford it, any way you slice it."

"But if you saw it . . ."

"Listen, the people there will be older—they'd all be on their second houses, and we're just starting out. There wouldn't be anybody our age there—you'd be all alone."

"But if you worked a little overtime and if I saved every penny, every single penny . . . think of the investment we'd have! And I don't care about friends . . ."

"You know, if your aunt would leave us something, we could make it without my taking so much overtime I get sick," he began, when the phone rang. We were waiting for the final call from the hospital where Aunt Ruth had been taken to die. The doctor said that with a constitution like hers, she could hang on forever, and we knew that it was only a matter of time before the scales were going to tip and Aunt Ruth's savings would be gone. Then our money would have to be dropped piece by piece down the deep black well, while we wished for her death. Whenever the phone rang at night, we were always tense, waiting for her.

"Maybe this is good news," Jack said, as he reached for it. It was the agent, calling to say that the smallest house in the neighborhood was up for sale, a bargain if we hurried.

We moved in the spring, and I put Toby in his bassinet down on my new doorstep. While I waited for Jack to bring the truck with our furniture, I tried to imagine really being there. There was a serenity in the empty room that was waiting for me—it was the full calm before the game begins, when your money is in neat piles of colors; when the players are all down on one clean nylon knee for the kickoff prayer. It was, for the moment, a fragile bridge between two worlds, that of their Mayflower van filled with cut velvet, which had just left, and that of the U-Haul filled with our Herculon, which was on its way. Suddenly, and finally, Aunt Ruth was gone, with all her aches and pains and complaints, like the dim night before;

she was swept away by the insistent sunshine of my new life in this neighborhood. She left us no money—in fact, the only thing I had from her was the dark quilt she had sewn in the last months she was alive, the only really creative thing I had ever seen her do. When she had gotten too sick to talk any more, she tore the dresses in her closet into pieces and then sewed and embroidered the shapes into a heavy, dreary quilt that didn't go with anything I owned. It was in the first box that would be carried into our new house because it was the last thing I had packed in the apartment, along with the other stuff I didn't know what to do about.

Perfection seemed quite tangible to me then as I looked in my empty new room. The sunlight was laid out in neat squares on the polished oak floors, sliced by the window frame into small lemon area rugs. I liked the room and the house better at that moment than I ever could again. It was the only time the room would have its own personality, a membrane thinly stretched across the pale floor, from white wall to fieldstone fireplace, and back to where I stood at the door. I knew I would destroy that delicate tissue once I stepped into it, like a bull charging through a paper hoop, and I knew the room would forever separate and spin backward, hanging in tatters on the horns of my own subjectivity once I entered it for the first time.

I wanted to empty my mind of everything but the sunlight, and for once to start new, to make the first page in this notebook look nice; to get rid of all the debris and memorabilia that cluttered everything. I wanted to lie down on the floor in the light and pretend I was swimming in water, on my flat stomach, the way I did when I was a kid and we could never go to a pool or to the beach because Aunt Ruth had to work all day. The only cool place in her apartment was the brown speckled linoleum on the living-room floor, so I used to lie on it, face down on the slick waxed surface, and pretend I was clinging to the sides of a giant trout in deep water. I was suspended, floating through the summers in lazy solitude above the hot sandwich shop where she stood at the counter, making hoagies and cheese steaks. Now, in the same way, I wanted to fall down into the inhuman emptiness of this new room as if it were a snowfall, to keep the furniture and Jack and Debbie and Toby from ever coming in to spoil the cleanness of it.

"You call this *clean?*"

I heard that voice cracking through my thoughts and backing into the room, and there she was again, sweating and scraping her bucket of brooms and rags in with her. "Okay. We can start over by the fireplace," she said, dropping to her knees.

And that was how I created the first of the many ghosts that were to haunt this house—the ghost that there can ever really be a beginning. I remember Aunt Ruth always used to say that all she ever wanted was peace and quiet. Then the rented truck that Jack didn't know how to drive screeched into the driveway, jerked forward, and stalled on the slope. I heard what was in there rock backward and settle against the barred tailgate as he jumped out and helped Debbie down. I could actually see the clean white silence in the living room splinter like a glass spider web and begin to fall all around me with the first clink of a Corning Ware casserole at the front door. When that first neighbor reached for my bell, I knew the Anvil Chorus had begun. Then I think I finally knew what Aunt Ruth meant, because I swear a splinter from that shattered glass web flew up and got stuck in my eye, and after that, everything began to look refracted and ugly.

My first visitor was a very short woman named Glynnis, who woke me from my nap to ask if I wanted to join the chapter of the American Association of University Women which was meeting at her house.

"We usually have a quick meeting on the second Tuesday of the month, and then we have different activities afterward. This month we have a speaker who's written a cookbook on the native food of Portugal," she began. "I'd like you to drop by for some coffee this Tuesday if you're interested. It will be a good chance to meet some of the women. You're not by any chance Portuguese, are you?"

This first invitation put me in the miserable position of telling a potato-shaped girl in a tasteless white leather jumper that I hadn't yet finished college. When she heard this, she wrinkled her upturned nose in what I think was the beginning of a smile, but instead caused her two cheek dimples to deepen. I could see my living room rise and fall in her square glasses, and her black fuzzy caterpillar brows crawled closer together as she blinked. Then she left, with hardly a glance around my newly decorated yellow living room, which I had set up as my major selling point for acceptance here.

Now, I certainly do plan to finish college someday, because I know that you go through life at the emotional level of whatever grade of school you last attended, joining the same groups, doing the same kinds of activities, again and again. And what's equally interesting is this—I've noticed that people will wear a variant of the style of clothing they wore in their last year of school for the rest of their lives, because that was when they felt the best about themselves. It's strange but true, and you don't have to be terribly perceptive to notice it. For example, Jack still wears khaki pants and loafers without socks, because he graduated from college in 1965; Glynnis's white leather jumper, on the other hand, was a variation of the Villager tweeds she had worn when she graduated from a New England girls' college in 1963. Her efficiency and assurance in walking up to the house of a total stranger on a rainy, blowy, private morning in April was obvious after graduating cum laude with a researching degree in Library Science. And my response—to retreat like a rumpled question mark into the kitchen for tea, wearing my dirty brown bathrobe and plaid babushka—was the direct result of getting only as far as my first semester of night school at an inner-city college in a disintegrating oil town on the Delaware River. And, like a disoriented freshman, thinking everybody cared.

It's always the same after first grade: in every group there is always the smartest one and the prettiest one, the popular one and the bad one, and I wondered who would hold these positions in this neighborhood. After Glynnis left, I filled the teapot and came back to the living room that she hadn't been interested in, and looked it over once more for possible flaws. I moved a little cup of strawflowers over to the table by the window, and as I did, I saw Glynnis stop short at her mailbox as a long Mercedes whizzed by the curb. It was going awfully fast on this carefully sleepy street and the wind that curled up behind it blew some of the mail out of Glynnis's hand onto the lawn. She turned her whole body sharply, like a fist, to stare at the car before she bent to pick up her mail. I moved three books over to the table next to the flowers so that the arrangement would look a little more intellectual, and waited to see if the car would come back up the street. The teapot whistled first, and I went in and made tea, checking my Salada fortune: "Life is what happens while you're making other plans." If there is reincarnation, I know Shakespeare is now writing for Salada. I brought my tea into the living room and sat in one chair and then another, checking on the look of the room from each one. If someone ever came over for coffee, I'd have her sit facing the fireplace. Just for insurance, I pulled the footstool over a little closer so she wouldn't have to lean so far to reach for the sugar. As far as I could see, my room looked inviting . . . I had everything set just so . . . now all I needed was a friend.

Unlike Glynnis, I personally would never miss the chance to look around someone else's living room for ideas, and I've even collected for the Mother's March of Dimes and gone Trick or Treating with the kids last year just to look in the entry foyers, halls, and living rooms of the other houses in the neighborhood. I know that Glynnis, for example, has gray wall-to-wall carpeting with a blue Chinese rug on top of it, and a small collection of delft on the mantel that she gathered herself from her year abroad, and she easily gets three times the mail that I do.

Sherry, our prettiest neighbor, is in the Junior League and always wears good jewelry. She has a house cleaner than the Avon Lady's, with a brilliant dewy kitchen floor that glows with an inner light. She has living-room curtains that match her Queen Anne fireplace chairs and two shy daughters that her decorator once said look like fine Madame Alexander dolls. I can see through the trees at the back of our property into her back yard, and on Wednesdays I've often talked across the line to Rosa, her cleaning lady, as she struggles to hang up Sherry's Princess Grace queen-sized sheets without letting them drag on the ground. When she bent into the laundry basket, I was close enough to see her bikini underpants through her beige stretch slacks, and they were decorated with a tiny black hand cupping each cheek. I once read somewhere, probably on a Salada tea bag, that a true sign of maturity is when you really know how to do something perfectly, yet you keep your mouth shut and let the other person learn for herself. One windy day before she was fired for ruining the laundry, Rosa paused over a slapping sheet, took a clothespin out of her mouth, and turned it slowly, as if it were a corncob pipe, before telling me, "Be careful. That big old house at the end of your street is up for sale." The big house is right next door to the Avon Lady and it has giant double front doors of paneled wood that are polished to a coffin sheen, lit at night with twin carriage lanterns. Rosa thinks everything important depends on what type of person owns the biggest house in a town.

Rosa was hired next by the Avon Lady, who looks like Doris Day with snow-white hair. She is president of the Neighborhood Alliance for Sports and Safety, and has a smooth slate foyer that she waxes. Through shuttered saloon doors I once saw her mahogany dining-room table, and it was completely covered with her tennis trophies. The next to the last time I ever wore the babushka was the day the Avon Lady came. I was trying to be dressed by ten o'clock or so, which was when Glynnis had first shown up and which was, I assumed, the beginning of proper visiting hours. But some days were harder than others. On that particular day I was planning to look as groomed as a secretary in the morning for Jack when he came home from work, so I'd rearranged my nap and Toby's bath and took my shower while he had his morning nap. Then, I put on the scarf after I'd washed and set my hair so that he wouldn't spit his milk onto the rollers. He used to have a sort of projectile form of colic, and the Avon Lady rang the doorbell just as he'd finished a long, warm breast of milk. She was wearing a white piqué dress with rose scallops at the neckline, like Tricia Nixon, and the bodice stood away from her body as if it were lined with shirt cardboard. Toby was beginning to doze and burp quiet dabs of oatmeal down my shoulder when she finally finished her presentation and tilted her wooden case closed with a smart rap that woke him up again. She turned the invoice warily toward us with a long, clean fingernail, and after I signed it, she wiped her pen off carefully before putting it back into her bag. Somehow she convinced me to buy four kinds of soap and perfume, and some sachet that came in a container shaped like a bunch of grapes, even though our payment booklet for the new furniture was as thick and dense as a slice of white bread.

A few months later, she left a big flowered bag of perfume in my mailbox and I found it stuffed in the back when I went out in the rain for the mail. A large ambulance, framed by a fine steady mist, was coming back up the street from the direction of the new house.

"Someone down the end of the street must have a serious problem," Glynnis said from under her neon-green slicker. The ambulance had been coming back and forth once every week, swiftly and silently, like the messages that were being circulated about it.

I took my Avon bag back into the house and put on some water for tea and looked around my kitchen with a stranger's eye to criticize the things a neighbor would see if one ever came into my house as far as the kitchen. A little spaghetti sauce had dribbled down the front of the stove and the cabinet doors were still only half painted. The begonias on the windowsill were dried out and dead, even though all the rain they would ever need was sliding, dribbling down the glass just inches in front of them. They were a species of *Begoniaceae tantalus* from my gardening neighbor, who lives on the other side of me. She has a harelip and a constant cold. She is secretary of the League of Women Voters, and she told me the begonias needed more water. This was on the day she brought over a sickly little plant and asked me to put it on a corner of my porch that gets a special slant of sun in the late afternoon, and then she asked if I would please bring it back if it started to revive. So I watered it and looked in my gardening encyclopedia for a clue to what it was, so we'd have something in common to talk about when she wanted it back. All I could be sure was that it wasn't something whose name began with *A* because so far I only had received volume one of *The Wonderful World of Plants*. This plant was covered with a dusty web of hairs or strings, and some of them were growing down the side of the pot, with an occasional bug or brown bead of growth on one of the strings. I turned it every day and I also brought all the begonias into my kitchen and put them at the window where I spend most of my time. The gardening neighbor spends most of her time in the greenhouse she built herself off of her kitchen window, where she eats endless green beans and reads garden catalogues and mystery novels. One day I carried over to her all the gory murder mysteries that the original owners of my house, a widow and her sister, had left behind in the basement. That was when she told me that a new, very mysterious woman was moving into the big house down the street.

"I think they're very eccentric," she said. "The wife is supposed to be an artist or something, and he's a doctor. Rosa thinks they're loaded. They've even had the house fumigated and it's almost brand-new." Her hair was pulled behind her ears, which were covered with fine, dark hairs, like a kiwi. She took a long bean string out of her teeth, laid it across the page she was reading, closed the book, and leaned forward. "I hear they're from California, which is too bad." I watched her stained, stubby fingers as she untied the pile of murder mysteries I'd brought her, and I realized that this opportunity might be the closest I could get to having a real friend in this neighborhood. You needed someone to talk to here, I was beginning to realize. People walked their babies in pairs, or played tennis in doubles, or shopped in car pools. She was separating the books into piles. "I think there's going to be something pretty fishy about the new couple. Don't ask me why—it's just a hunch, but I can feel it in my bones," she said. "Here—these I've already read." She began binding up half the pile to give back. "The one about the Moors murders is great! Gives details. I need your finger . . ." While I held down the knot she was tying tightly around and under my index finger, she said, "Frankly, I never trust anyone under thirty, and I haven't been wrong so far." I thought it best not to tell her I was twenty-three, and didn't. The knot squeezed smoothly off my fingertip. The leaves of the Wandering Jew in the basket above her head waved gently in the soft breeze from the greenhouse fan, and I realized she could see through the Dieffenbachia along the wall into my own empty window to the brown begonias dying there. And she could probably see me in there, too.

I can't tell you how upset it gets me when a plant I've tried to grow starts to die. I consider it a sign of my personal worthlessness—that not even a measly begonia will succeed for me. These in particular were especially demanding, which is why I put them near the sink. I trimmed them, and thinned them, and finally put them into deep saucers to hold extra water, but still they lost limbs each day like lepers. Then I did a terrible thing to them that still worries me: once I saw them wilting, looking ugly, slipping, I stopped trying to keep them alive. I stopped watering them, but meanwhile, pretended to be concerned, and so they had no choice then but to die, because I had determined to kill them off once they showed weakness. I thus eliminated the element of suspense and gave myself at least the power of death over them. This worries me, of course, and that's because I am a mother.

Nurturing is my business. I brought my tea to the table in the corner of my kitchen and sat down in my chair, which allows me to have my back against the wall so that I can see out of two different windows, and three if I bend around. I am like a giant eye when I'm sitting there in my chair. I can see what is going on on two different streets outside, for a total of six houses, as well as who is coming up on my back porch. I can see Toby crawling around the corner after his nap, Debbie at the bus stop, and anyone else coming into the kitchen, pet or person, including my aunt, who strolls in each morning just as I settle down with my second cup of tea. She berates me for my laziness. She knows I keep the same sheets on the bed for months, and then vacuum the grit off them, rather than change them. She knows I eat most of the hot dog and give Toby the roll for lunch, and that I have never washed my hairbrush since I moved away from her. And she doesn't approve. My worst grades in school were always in self-control, and ironically, that's the one quality you need if you're going to stay home for a living.

The only other place to sit in the kitchen is by the phone. Now, if the phone rings, it is important always to sound busy. If I've been taking a nap, I will still climb out of bed and go into the kitchen to talk on the phone there, so that I can wake up a little on the way, rather than just reach across the bed for the phone. It is very important never to admit that you were taking a nap. Before I was married, Art, my boss, used to call home to his wife at different times of the day to catch her, and then when he hung up, he'd always take the shredded end of the cigar out of his mouth and say, "Damn! All she ever does is sleep." Everyone in the office would look up and there she'd be in the middle of us, stretching and yawning under the fluorescent lights, a creature from another world with pillow creases scarring her cheeks like a Yoruba maiden. When I finally met her at a party, even though her hair was neat and shiny and her eyes were clear, I looked at her with the cynical reserve I feel for alcoholics in new suits. With no warning at all, I expected her to reel over to the couch and sleep it off.

You see, the big problem with staying home is the lush, sensual thickness of the job, which can be more dangerous to the alert than a dreamy lotus field stretching into the haze. I think my problem with being frigid began after Debbie was a baby and only got worse when Toby was born. I can physically love these babies so much more than I can love Jack—they are softer, rubbed with oils; they always smile when I come to pick them up and cling like monkeys to my neck, full of Johnson & Johnson's finest perfumes. So whenever you answer the phone at home, you must lie convincingly about what it is you've been doing. I've learned through experience that you can sleep only if you're coming down with something; eat only if you're tasting dinner; read, only rarely, by first mentioning that you've already done three loads of wash and are merely waiting for the rinse cycle; masturbate, never.

Now, after the orientation period of that first summer, it was obvious that the women in this neighborhood were all of life's seniors and graduate students, and I felt left out, bruised, called upon only to perform errands and baby-sit scraggly plants. I was grateful when September finally came to begin shutting me in for the winter. On this particular morning Debbie, who still seemed like a piece of me, was waiting at the bus stop for her kindergarten bus and I was therefore more concerned at the window than ever, watching her. I had been in the neighborhood for five months now and still hadn't made a single friend, so the phone never rang and my day was very quiet, but it was the quiet of neglect, of the world keeping away. It was going to be a cold rainy September, the *Farmer's Almanac* predicted, perfect for sleeping, and all the windows were already closed, trapping the weather outside. Every sound was muffled. It's funny, but when the leaves fall and the windows close, you can see so much farther. I can add three or four more houses to my line of vision, but it seems a little unreal because I hear less. Then just the opposite thing happens in the spring, when the leaves block the view and through the open windows you can hear voices, preternaturally near, but unseen. This effect is what makes Zhivago foolhardy and desperate as he runs over the dreaming snow and keeps Ramar wily and cautious as he creeps through the whispering underbrush.

The rain was falling lightly and the closed screen behind the window was full of raindrops, making a Mondriaan pattern of rainbow squares that reflected my face again and again, as if I were looking into a giant faceted bee's eye. While my tea was cooling, I tilted back in my chair past the dead begonias, and moved the green gingham curtain aside a little so I could see more clearly up to the end of the street, where the bus would enter the neighborhood. A brown spider that was hidden in a fold in the curtain was shaken loose and dropped down in front of me onto the pane of glass and then pulled itself back up to its web in the corner. The web vibrated, the spider curled up tight, and I sipped my tea, waiting, when suddenly I saw in the drops what looked like a hundred women walk up to Debbie at the bus stop. I blinked away the bee vision and saw the real Maggie for the first time, framed by the wooden spokes of the window, and I knew then and there that I would have just one last chance to make a friend in this neighborhood.

I watched as she parked her stroller at the bus stop under the branches of a tree, and I estimated that she was my age or younger, because she was wearing her reddish hair in two pigtails that stuck out from under her yellow halo of a rainhat like the rays a child will draw coming out of the sun with an orange crayon. She was also wearing jeans and a pea jacket, which placed her in college in the late sixties. She looked too thin to be friendly, and I ordinarily never bothered with people with red hair because they seem just a little unpeeled, but on the other hand, I couldn't be all that choosy. If I could get to her before the other women did, if I could just get dressed in time and get out to the bus stop before she left, then everything would work out.

I jumped up from the table and moved away from my window and my tea, elbowed past Aunt Ruth, who was mutely rubbing in disgust at the spaghetti mess on the stove, and then I was running past the dining room, where out the window I saw her looking into Debbie's rain-pinged lunch box, ripping off my slippers and babushka as I went. It was like high school, even grade school, all over again, but it always is, and always will be throughout life. In spite of everything I've done since that afternoon, I know I'll always have to work hard to get friends, and worse, I'll always have to work against extraordinary obstacles. Like now; as I was running down the hall, my raised foot and slipper caught on Toby's tomato-pumper fire truck, on which I rolled forward for a long split second until I was stopped by the small but antique table which held my gargoyle, and it flew off and crashed against Toby's door, and the piece of the wing that chipped off in a knife wedge was the one that sliced into the soft part of my palm when I fell on it. The truck, propelled by the push, moved away from me backward down the hall with a clicking sound, with the driver's tomato head shaking from side to side.

I hate pain. I really hate pain. I feel so chastised, and invariably it's because I was doing something wrong at the time: getting too close, trying too hard, going too fast. The whole point in living is to figure out how to skate and slide and duck around the burrs of the real world without getting hit. And pain always throbs with a hellish wrapping hug—and it always forces you to know that the real world indeed has identity, with pain as its gritty, pebbly calling card. Aunt Ruth says the more pain you have, the more you can stand. That the world is full of pain, make no mistake.

There was no mistaking the real world now as I huddled there in the hall. My blood was shiny on the wall, but nearly black on the plaid babushka, which had ripped in two when I fell. And then suddenly Toby cried out and began to clatter his leg brace against the side of the crib, and there was more throbbing and spurts on the way to the bathroom, where I tried to stop the bleeding before I ruined the sink and floor that I had already cleaned up once that day. Then the back door blew open with a gust of wind and rain and Debbie dropped her metal lunch box on the floor as the school bus squealed off its air brakes and pulled away without her.

"That lady out there says our classes are changed all this week to afternoon because of conferences," she said.

"Stay away or I'll bleed on you and ruin your new dress," I said weakly. It's amazing how having little children forces you to sound like John Wayne sometimes. "What time this afternoon? Did the lady say?"

"Twelve-thirty. She said be back at the bus stop at twelve-thirty."

That gave me three hours to get ready.

"Mommy, she is really pretty! You should see . . . hey, what's that? EEEuuuuuuuuyuck look at your fingers . . . eeeeuuuuuu, you've got *blood* all over your nightgown!"

"Debbie, help your brother out of the crib and turn on the

TV set . . . here—wait—take the top off this bottle for me, and then go get your brother . . ."

I knew the gargoyle had been made in some hot country where it was probably cured over a camel-dung fire, so my first idea after making a tourniquet from my Hers towel was to try and bubble out some of the pottery crumbs with peroxide, so that my hand wouldn't rot off. I hate foreign objects in my body.

"Mommy, are you gonna come out to the bus stop with me and meet the lady?"

Toby's screams, now that Debbie was running between his crib and the bathroom with messages, were coming in spurts, along with my blood, making an appropriate horror-movie background. Horror movies really bother me, especially their great dependence on irony. Here, for example, in this particular Monday-morning horror movie, I insisted on buying the weird gargoyle, which I then mysteriously tripped over, and which is now in my palm, and maybe, now, I AM THE GARGOYLE!!!

"Mommy! The lady wants to see you, she said! She's Riva's mother and she lets her wear ballet shoes to school."

Maybe my insides are beginning to harden, even now, my organs turning into brittle lumps of clay, my arteries into pottery . . . I'm a little teapot, short and stout . . .

"The lady says I can take dancing lessons with Riva, if you say yes. It's on Saturday . . ."

First, I'll notice a stark grayness around my eyes, then harsh lines will appear until I'm a shrunken apple face on a hunched-over body with a proclivity for the top of the downspout . . .

"All I need is two leotards and practice slippers, she said. Please say yes, say yes, please!"

Each time I looked up from the blood, Debbie was a voice in Toby's room, and now she was back at the bathroom door, this time dragging him, still in his brace, as he sucked on his blanket for breath. He was screaming limply every now and then as she propped him against the clothes hamper, and then she climbed up on the tub to watch me closer.

"You should see the lady's baby," she began, and then stopped when she saw the cut, now with all the blood bleached out.

"Mommy! That's really sickening! Put some Band-Aids on it! That lady says she wants to meet you, and her baby can play with Toby. She said she's got a bean-bag chair in her house."

Now ordinarily I try to avoid using Band-Aids as much as possible, because they only prolong the inevitable pain of exposure. "Make yourself tough," Aunt Ruth always used to say. "Then nothing can hurt you." But I had to use Band-Aids and cover this cut up because it looked so ugly—just like one of my stuffed pork chops, where I slice into the soft pink meat in the middle of the chop, lift up the flap, and stuff some bread crumbs in between.

"Why don't you go eat your Tastykake from your lunch box while I take a bath," I suggested to Debbie over the running water. "And bring Toby some toys."

I always put the hamper in front of the door to keep Anthony Perkins out and to keep Toby in so he won't put a fork in an electrical outlet while I'm in the tub. I'm sure Debbie can be trusted for the ten minutes or so that I'm under water. Of course, there are always the exceptions—I read in the paper where a mother was taking a shower and her four-year-old was playing with matches and burned the whole house down all around the poor woman, except for the shower, where she was still standing when the firemen came. They always make it a point to tell you in those stories what the mother was doing wrong—she just ran to the store for a pack of cigarettes—she just dozed off for a minute—she was talking on the phone when the kid, who was jumping on the bed, flew out of the tenth-story window. So I simply keep the kids with me all the time. And I'm afraid I do read a lot, all the time, every chance I get. I was the second smartest in grade school, and by high school, the nuns thought it was such a shame that I couldn't go to college, in this day and age, but we needed the money, so I got a job.

I used to like to bathe alone. It was the only time I could be sure of some privacy, because as long as she thought I was cleaning myself, Aunt Ruth wouldn't bother me in the bathroom.

"Can I watch you take a bath? I can eat my Tastykake in here—it's already wet from the rain when I opened my lunchbox to show Riva's mother what I had to eat . . ."

Riva's mother, Riva's mother! I can't even think about myself, alone here in the bathroom, without Riva's mother crowding in. I used to like to fill the tub with the hottest water I could get into, and then play and read there, content even without a shower massage, secure in the knowledge that Aunt Ruth would do anything not to have to look at my nicely budding body floating naked in the suds and just about 99 44/100's percent as pure. She used to say she could see an invisible film of dirt on everything, even if no one else could, so she expected me to take a long time in the tub. I used to imagine that the other 56/100's percent part that wasn't so pure was so unnamefully filthy, so black and sticky and tarlike, so rotten and festering and licorice, that all the washing in the world didn't matter. Nothing would ever clean it up, change it, take it away, except to ignore it, pretend it didn't exist; which is why they had to take Marilyn Chambers off the Ivory Soap box. Officially, of course, this part is called Original Sin: unofficially, I thought it might be something like a swirl of fudge ripple through vanilla ice cream.

I remember the last bath I took in Aunt Ruth's house before I got married, when the more I thought about Jack and the wedding, the more I scrubbed, until my back and the bottoms of my feet were raw. Jack told me later that he did the same thing, spit-shining his army shoes until he wore a hole in the handkerchief he was using to rub them with. He even polished the soles, because he knew he'd be kneeling up there at the altar in front of his captain from the reserves, and so everyone saw the shiny soles and I was the only one who could see that his index finger on the white satin kneeler was still completely black from the indelible shoe polish.

That's how it's always been with Jack—to an observer, there is never anything you could find wrong with him—it is his job to have no obvious flaws, because first he must sell himself, and then the anti-pollution devices. It is only when he comes home that he is allowed to husk off the dusty shoes and peel off his sweaty socks; to pick at the pimples that will be gone by morning; to exchange a stained, wrinkled suit for another one that isn't. If he falls into bed exhausted at six-thirty in the evening, he will nonetheless be up and glowing with good health at six-thirty the next morning. I see the detritus and the calluses, of course, and the secretaries and clients see the crisp Rooster tie dangling under his nearly effortless smile.

It was his smile that sold me—he has had only two fillings in his life—and when he said, "Let's do it, let's get hitched up!" I did it, even though Aunt Ruth needed my paychecks more than she wanted to be rid of me, I think. I felt the same way then about getting married that I feel now when I'm considering buying something I really want but don't think we can afford: it's a risk, but you can only move ahead with a risk.

"Is Daddy flying yet?" Debbie asked, from under the sink, where she was reading.

"He's been up for about ten minutes now."

"Did you pray him up?"

"Of course I did." I'm not crazy. While I was cleaning my hand, I pictured his airplane rising safely through the steely rain and shooting him into Indianapolis. Even though I hate being alone again and again, I always synchronize my watch with his before he leaves and then think him aloft about the time of his takeoff, just for luck. As it happened this morning, he took off at 9:25 a.m., at precisely the moment when the blue deodorant Dial squeezed out of my good hand like a wet watermelon seed and plodded flat against the floor by the sink, and I suddenly realized in horror, from the tub, that he was still there, in the soap under the pipes by Debbie's lunch box.

"Debbie, sweetie, could you hand me the soap there by you?" I asked her casually enough. She put the soap into the back of Toby's melon dumper and rolled it over to the tub, without looking up from her book. I rubbed the hairs off it and tried to calm my panic at being alone again.

I had already wiped his urine and curly pubic hairs off the white rim of the toilet and slammed the seat down, where it would stay for the week. The first day alone is always the hardest, until his toothbrush dries. When I rinsed his whisker peppers out of the sink for the last time that week, I forgave him for leaking, and when I swished his blood and red-polka-dot toilet-paper patches down the drain, I forgave him for leaving, I think. I lifted his plane safely above the Philly smog and let him float away to make money for us in peace. That was our agreement, the first of the unspoken Golden Great Truths that we created when we got married. I should support him in supporting us, and I do. Gamely, cheerfully, bravely, creatively, unrelentingly. My first job is to take care of him so he can take care of us. What he doesn't know, of course, is that I have rules of my own as well, my stainless-steel ones, the first of which is that I would have agreed to anything with him just to be able to get out of the house and away from Aunt Ruth.

Now, of course, there is really no getting away from Aunt Ruth, except in the bath, so I stay in the water as long as possible, rather than face her somewhere else in the house. Once on *Hawaii Five-o*, they tortured McGarrett by totally depriving him of all sensory stimulation, sort of the opposite of a think tank, I would imagine. They blindfolded him, plugged up his ears, stripped him naked, and shaved him all over, and then floated him in a tank of still water that was heated to precisely 98.6 degrees. Have I forgotten any senses? His nose was clamped into an oxygen unit, and the point was that, with no sensory information coming new and fast from the outside world, he would smoothly go crazy and tell all his secrets to Wo Fat, the enemy.

"Men have to keep moving, or they go crazy," Jack is always telling me, and so we found a pediatrician who would give Toby a brace to sleep in that would force his legs to grow straight, because Jack reasoned that if Toby can't walk straight, he won't be able to run. On the other hand, I think that slow, hardly perceptible movement has its own kind of thrill, too; like when I'm in my car in the parking lot and the car beside me starts to pull out and I have the sudden moment of fear that it's me that's moving, rolling backward into the street. Jack may like the whir and hum of a spinning top, but I like the slow blurry picture that comes crawling off it when someone is pumping it at top speed. Einstein was right, napping on the deck of his sailboat there in the calm and saying that here was spin enough for him—it's all relative.

It's all in how you look at it, I've discovered. Perspective is one of the most important things in life. It helps me not to feel sorry for myself when Jack leaves if I look at my situation from different angles. Sometimes I think I'm pinned down here like a caught insect, stuck to this empty house while he flies free above the clouds, and sometimes I'm grateful for the privacy away from another adult that these weeks alone give me, although God knows I get a little spooky from the solitude after a while. When I was taking my last unmarried bath, I put in enough bubble solution to last the whole bath, I thought, and I also thought Jack and I would share everything after that night. But when he started going away for whole weeks at a time, I couldn't cope with the volume of unshared words that piled up, and to tell him everything would take weeks and weeks. So a pocket of privacy was created, the way the soap makes the bubbles die out and you have a hole of water in the bath. Now I'm afraid if I get too much more privacy, that the very consistency of the thing we're sitting in is going to change, as each week alone eats into the bubbly dream I used to have of honeymoon togetherness. Yet I've always liked being alone more than anything. When Aunt Ruth knocked on the bathroom door to hurry me along, I used to want to go swimming down the drain with the escaping bath water, leaving only my dirty clothes behind. To go away and see new worlds and not have to wash the dishes any more.

Now it wasn't as if I had it all that bad growing up—not at all. It's just that the life I did have fell so short of all the other lives I saw. In my reader, the little girl always wore clean ankle socks that never got stuck down on her heel, her school had a cafeteria and she had money to buy little bowls of red Jell-O, and she had a young mother who wore pearls and was happy to see her come home. The mother on *Lassie* baked peanut-butter cookies while Jeff went out berry-picking . . . I could go on and on, but what's the use? Like everybody else, I find myself pulling away from my own past with a hard look in my eye. I know I should be grateful that I had an aunt who cared enough to raise me when nobody else would, who gave up her life as a single woman when she was too old to really bother to share all her free time with a troublesome child, to go to work to support me, and where's the law that says if one kid wears monogrammed cashmere sweaters to college, everybody else should? And look how lucky I am now, to have a house and family in this nice, tree-lined neighborhood, to have my health—enough! I believe! In it all! I should never have eaten the hot dog, I should never have dozed off and left the kids unattended or bought the Avon stuff. I should have stayed with Aunt Ruth and worked and not gotten married. And I'm a rotten ingrate who's been in the bathtub too long, feeling sorry for myself, and all I've got to show for it is five white raisins for fingertips on my good hand and a smoky sauna for a bathroom. Okay, okay, I'll be good . . .

"Mom! Mommy! Toby's drinking out of the bathtub again, and you didn't see him."

Let me just draw a window here on this fogged-up bathroom mirror so I can see what there is to work with. I'll wipe the fog away, and the past away, too . . . Except for one more little thing that this mirror reminds me of, the thing I wanted the most and now can never have because I don't believe in it any more. It was a Winky Dink screen. God, did I want a Winky Dink screen.

When I think about it, I really did have a deprived childhood, but everybody needs a childhood deprived of certain essentials so that they can look for them when they grow up, making life a long scavenger hunt. I probably wouldn't be the kind of person I am today if I had been tucked gently into kindergarten like the other kids, playing, as I imagined they did, with a hundred Lincoln Logs on a red carpet in the sunlight, instead of stretching out full length, as I did, on the cold gray concrete stoop of our apartment building when it was my turn to be patient for Richard Murphey.

I had a deprived childhood and nothing will ever make up for the things I missed. My bones are set now, and I'm too big and clumsy for dancing lessons to do any good. The rabbit hole through which you crawl to follow the yellow speckled summer-afternoon laughter at Camp Winnie Ha-Ha has winked shut, and I no longer believe in the magic that by coloring in some lines I will change anything for Winky Dink. You see, you had to draw with a crayon on a piece of plastic film that you spread over your TV screen and you could then create certain real props in the cartoon story, like a bridge between two mountaintops, a wobbly arc that Winky Dink would run across and, with your help, he could escape the baddies.

If you didn't have a Winky Dink screen, what you did have instead was the inescapable knowledge that Winky Dink was a fake. You never drew the bridge in . . . yet he still ran across.

"Use your imagination, it's free," Aunt Ruth used to say, walking past the TV set with her hangers full of ironed shirts.

But I don't want to talk about this any more, or stay in this bathroom any more. There is something about Winky Dink that bothers me more than nearly anything else I can imagine, but I'll think about it some other time, or forget about it, because it's starting to give me a headache.

"This isn't hard to hold!" . . . Debbie was picking up the can of hair spray and putting it down, picking it up and putting it down.

Wait a minute! It was common sense! That was the sense I forgot in the McGarrett story. Wo Fat couldn't plug that one up, and the slippery McGarrett floated free.

By an hour later that afternoon, the rain had stopped and the sun was coming out in spots, dappling the windowpane. That was too bad, actually, because I had already created a fantasy of just how I was going to meet Maggie: two strangers, we'd be separated by splintering sheets of rain and we'd steer through the glistening mists with the wet prows of our baby strollers to join hands over the children's heads in a rainbow of friendship, I thought. But by the time I dressed Toby up in two sweaters and his nor'easter hat, Debbie was sweating under her raincoat and the rain had stopped, the birds had started squeaking and chirping, and the sun kept flashing out, then disappearing. To make matters worse, the gardening neighbor saw me as I was unfolding Toby's stroller on the side porch and waved her trowel at me before I could pretend I hadn't seen her. She had been kneeling at the edge of her garden, digging up potatoes, and if the stroller hadn't rusted closed in the rain, I might have been able to open it up and get out to the bus stop alone, before she ever saw me. But from my crouching position beside the stroller, I could see her stand up and brush the mud off her knee pads and by the time I broke the hinge off and opened up the stroller, she was already cutting across my side yard, stuffing her gardening gloves into her jacket as she walked. She was wearing toilet plungers on her knees.

"Hi, y'all!" she said, rattling the screen door that I'd just locked when I saw her coming. She'd told me her name before, and I couldn't remember it now. I wanted to write "Go away" in the dust on the porch floor, but instead I smiled and said hello without getting up.

"Knock, knock . . . it's locked," she said, rattling the door again, and Debbie ran over and pushed up the latch. "I hardly ever see you outside," she said, and when she stepped up to the porch, the plungers dimpled and puckered against her chinos. She saw me staring. "You'd be surprised how comfortable they are . . . I even forget I'm wearing them sometimes," she said. "They last for years."

"Did you buy them somewhere?" I asked, listening for the bus to enter the neighborhood and hearing, instead, the tiny high-pitched squeal that meant I was getting a headache.

"Heck no—I made them myself! A couple of straps from the five-and-ten, twist out the wooden handles, of course, but that's common sense—anyone could do it— Hey, wait—am I keeping you from something? You all look so spiffy! What's the celebration?"

"Mommy's going to talk to the new lady at the bus stop," Debbie said before I could. "She's been getting cleaned up the whole morning. She's got her new knee socks on, from Korvette's. Like mine. Mine are white. Mommy's are brown."

"Well then! This must certainly be a red-letter day for all of you," the gardening neighbor said. "C'mon—I'll walk you to the bus stop, keep you company while you wait. I'd like to meet this person myself."

"Goodie, goodie!" Debbie started. "We can all play hopscotch."

"*You* can play hopscotch, *I* have to rock Toby so he doesn't scream and wake up the whole neighborhood," I said.

"Spoil-sport! You never play with me—you always have to rock that stupid creepy baby. Nobody ever plays with me."

"C'mon, kid, if I can remember how it goes, you've got yourself a game," the gardening neighbor said, and Debbie ran into her room for chalk as we started down the street. When we got there, the giant tree was still dripping from the rain, and it seemed as if even the weather had gotten excited at seeing me outside and uncovered, there on the corner. The sun was showing off for my benefit, flashing in my eyes until they watered, making my headache worse. I kept staring down the street in the direction of Maggie's house, watching for her so I'd be the first to spot her. But it also meant that I was staring directly into the sun, and the dappled light that was glittering off the millions of drops of rain on the thousands of wandering leaves on the tree above my head was shooting into my eyes with a machine-gun staccato and beating tempo with the changing wind. And each time the sun came out full blast, it would turn the windows in my kitchen, which I could see clearly from where I stood, into burning squares of white fire. They were burning like welder's flames, too bright to look directly into, and I felt as if I were melting down there on the pavement, under a magnifying glass that tilts to catch the sun in a laser beam.

And then, when the wind lifted and softened, there would come this unbelievably sickening smell of vomit, which would get worse with each back-and-forth movement I gave Toby's stroller, keeping time with Debbie's singing, keeping him asleep. Who could stand this smell? And where did it come from? I looked warily at the gardening neighbor, who was kneeling on the sidewalk a few feet away, drawing hopscotch for Debbie. Was it here earlier when Maggie stood here? Did she make it? It wasn't coming from Toby—I felt into his diaper and he was clean for as far as I could stick my finger—so where was it coming from?

"Does your bus stop always smell this bad?" I called to Debbie, who was plowing big piles of leaves at the curb into the storm drain. She didn't hear me—now that she's big enough to walk away, she does.

Was it coming from me?

She was singing as she pushed piles of leaves ahead of her with her new saddle shoes, piles wet and heavy as giant tea bags.

Singing: "The eensy weensy spider went up the spider spout . . ."

I always had to wear saddle shoes to school, and it's interesting, considering how many ways I invented to rip the soles off of them, to think that now I see them as the prettiest shoes a kid can wear, and so I keep buying new pairs for Debbie each time she grows out of the old ones.

The gardening neighbor joined in the singing: "Down came the rain, and washed the spider out . . ."

It's funny, but once you own a house, you start noticing all those little things like rainspouts, and where the rain runs as it leaves the roof. Rather than sitting by the window and watching the rain coming down, now I worry if the rainspout is clear of dead leaves and will it carry the rainwater away from the basement so the boxes with my Ben Casey and Dr. Kildare collections won't get soaked and ruined. I wish I were back home by my window right now, instead of under this dribbling tree.

"Out came the sun, and dried up all the rain," they sang together. It's awful being splatted by these last drops of wind spit once it's stopped raining, and they always hit me right on top of my head where I've parted my hair. And this miserable, pukey smell that's here—I should be home. The reason I most hate to go outside is that I've always been afraid of the wind. I'm ashamed to admit it, but it's true. Personally, I prefer there to be a pane of glass between me and the wind, so that by seeing what's hitting the glass, instead of me, I can safely see what's usually invisible.

"Come on, Mommy—sing the spider song."

"Sing, sing! And the eensy weensy spider came up the spout again!"

Up, down, back, forth—with each line of the song, with each rock of the stroller, each step in the hopscotch, and each car that swished by, I could feel my thoughts shift and bend, turn and fold back, and I saw my scene of a rainbow friendship with Maggie fly away like an origami bird. She probably isn't even coming . . . and if she does, she'll probably think I made the bus stop this stinky. It's funny, I thought I really knew all about this bus stop because I'd watched it for hours and hours from my kitchen window, and yet I didn't know the most important thing about it—this comprehensive quality that completely obliterates all the others—this stink, this horribly rotten smell. I'm as bad as my begonias dying at the window—just a sliver of glass away from the real thing.

I really get bored with the outside, because there's never anything to do except look around. Nature is so messy, especially after a rain. There is mud splashed up on the sidewalk, wet soggy leaves and twigs have fallen everywhere, and the street mail, what little there is in a neighborhood like this, is ruined. I should tell the gardening neighbor about street mail—it would give her something else to do beside draw lines on the sidewalk with Debbie, but I know what her reaction would be—she'd think I'm as weird as she is.

"Did I hear you correctly? Did you say 'street mail'?" Jack asked me when I first told him. He really doesn't think I'm all that normal—he's just about come right out and said as much. I can't decide whether to try and act normal and dull for his benefit, or to spice things up for both of us by telling him some real dirt. In fact, if I don't get over this little problem of being frigid, he's told me I should seriously consider seeing a psychiatrist. I figure that sort of thing would cost about the same as a new bedspread and curtain set for our bedroom, which would certainly cheer me up a little. Then, depending on how crazy I turn out to be, we could buy a new rug, or even a brass bed with the same amount of money. It's all the same to Jack, he said, because he's on the road so much that he just wants to be comfortable when he comes home.

But the street-mail thing is authentic; I can vouch for it. It's one of those things in life that are based on the premise that you have nothing to lose, like Pascal's theory about believing in God: you might as well, because if there is a God, then you're covered; if not, what's it matter? Who's to care? It's the same thing with street mail. In this world of infinite possibilities, countless permutations (of course I'm not crazy—this is the language of a sane person), and multiple choice, there is a chance that there is no chance.

I mean, what have you got to lose? If you don't believe in this theory, you simply have the regular litter of the world around you. If you do believe in it, you have street mail, personally addressed to you. Paper clips mean you should be collecting something, tying up loose ends, making some kind of connection between things. I usually find a paper clip when I feel that my world is coming apart, or a straight pin will say the same thing, since that's a masculine paper clip. Money is clearly and simply a reward, always showing the true worth of any job that you've recently completed. I always find money when I clean the house; for example, sometimes two cents in the bottom of the washing machine, a quarter in the couch cushion, a nickel when I weed. God does not believe in a minimum wage, of course, and remember, you can find street mail everywhere—inside as well as outside. Book markers and holy cards are inspirational, and reading other people's marketing lists and unpaid bills is an important way of finding a common denominator in the human condition. Mittens and winter hats are the way God takes care of you—you just pick them up and wash them, and you're warm—remember the lilies and the birds never needing to buy clothes? If you happen to see a lot of the same kind of thing drifting by, bottle caps or rubber bands, for instance, and you can't see any reason for picking them up and yet you can't get over how many of these things you see, then it's simply a metaphoric message about something very particular to your life and you just have to file it away until you make some sense of it. God loves to hide behind a metaphor.

Being sensitive to street mail makes you look at life as if it were a game in which you have an active role and the clues to your next move are always right there in front of you. You simply have to learn how to read them. But you must never try to force the game along—the best thing you can do is to ask for a new piece of mail when you're needing some direction and then promise that you'll read it and abide by it when it comes. Sometimes abiding by it is the more difficult part of this bargain, especially when the message says to stop doing something that feels really good.

Unfortunately, as I said, the rain had wrecked the possibility of any mail on this corner, so I was left merely to look around me, rather than do something concrete. Jack and I are alike on this—we both hate to just look at the outside. On our last vacation to Canada, I noticed that we were never content to just look out the car window at the scenery rolling by. No, we had to talk about owning it, reproducing something like it in our own back yard, or try to take it home by taking pictures of it, drawing it, writing about it, or even pressing pieces of it in the AAA Travel Guide. Perhaps it's because we're just starting out in adult life that we want to take things —maybe maturity is when you can admire something for itself and not want it for yourself. Or maybe you grow up when you stop taking and start giving back.

And I wasn't finished being mad at Jack, I realized, while I stood there in the shooting sunlight and the vomit fumes. Little thoughts of revenge because he was gone again kept imploding inside my head like dumdum bullets every time I saw any station wagon like ours pass by on the main road. I thought of Jack's flat hands, hairless on the steering wheel, and the balding back of his head as he drove away. I ignore the baldness except when I'm mad at him, and then it's the first in the long list of things I think about that encourages me not to care if we stay together or not.

Such a list is important—it keeps things in perspective. Another thing I do is watch him talk with his head upside down in my lap. He thinks I'm being very loving and attentive as he lies there and talks, but what I'm actually doing is watching his lower jaw move in and out, protruding and distorted, and it's a simple matter then to think he's homely and alien.

"Mommy! You should see your face—it's all white with two big red circles on your cheeks!"

"I don't feel so well, Deb. Mommy's getting a little cold," I lied, taking out my pocket compact to look at my face. I never tell her about these headaches—I don't want them to be hereditary. She was right about the cheeks, though.

"Are you gonna throw up?" she asked, jumping in place.

In the corner of the mirror I saw a new car turn into our development, while I rubbed at my Natural Wonder blusher to get some of it off. I tipped the mirror over to watch Debbie —she was easier to deal with when I had a headache if I put her into the mirror, but she and the gardening neighbor had done their final hop out of my line of mirror vision and had moved over beside me as the car slowly approached. We were lined up, waiting, like the last lonely members of a Cargo Cult while the shiny car came closer.

"I'm sweaty hot!" Debbie was saying, peeling off her raincoat. "You should be a horse, Mommy."

"Whew!" the gardening neighbor said. "It's the berries."

"Why, for God's sake?" I asked, but all conversation was suspended as the car, a cream-colored Mercedes, rolled up close to us and stopped. I looked down at it and saw my own face rolling out of sight as the window smoothly disappeared into the cream door, and then in place of me I saw the most handsome male face I think I've ever seen in my life up close.

"Hi!" Debbie said.

"Hubba, hubba!" whispered the gardening neighbor, rubbing her plungers together.

I could tell by his clothes that here was no ordinary college graduate of, say, 1964 to 1966. This was the Ivy League! Smiling, of course, and he was wearing my favorite color of blue Oxford cloth, a button-down-collared shirt which was loosened at the neck, and a brown plaid tie that was fatly knotted and pulled over to one side. Blue, rolled-up sleeves, dark hairy arms, one bent elbow up and out of his window, the other curved on the back of the empty passenger seat, and unfortunately for me, I pictured it curved around my shoulders, which is probably where all the trouble began, as I look back.

His brown corduroy jacket was folded beside him on the seat, because it was getting warm with the sun out. I wanted him to take me home, away from all this, and his legs were open and bent softly, and I could see the shape of his raised knee under the worn tan fabric. He had brown curly hair and perfect white teeth, blue-tinted, horn-rimmed aviator sunglasses, long fingers, and I think he said something about had the bus come yet?

"No," Debbie said, and the gardening neighbor's whispered "*Who*, who is *he*?" floated up into the trees.

He was somebody's father, Hunk or Chunk, I think he said, brown leather belt with a brass buckle on it like the kind that used to be on the old Flagg Flier shoes—one flip and it's opened, and I rarely notice such details, it's just that with a headache coming on, I'm usually more sensitive—thin lips, very thin, hair curling around his earlobes, music and pipe smoke curling out and around his window and past my hair, and arms . . . And then he rolled the window back up, my face was back on the glass, and he was gone, leaving me up to my knees in vomit fumes. The gardening neighbor's voice trailed after him, wrapped around the cream rear end of his car like the moan after an ambulance. "Wow," she said, as the car went down the street under an arbor of trees and disappeared. I looked up and saw that the trees there were shades of red and yellow. Had they just done that, or were they like that yesterday? Since I couldn't see them from my kitchen window, it looked as if they had just blushed and lit up when he passed under them. I looked down and saw that I was standing in a pinkish, yellowish pulp that, if it wasn't my emotions made flesh, must have dropped out of the tree above my head. A few berries, dull and about the size of fat, rotting Bing cherries, had fallen into Toby's stroller while he slept. They were mashed like chewing gum on the sole of my shoe.

It was a real housewife shoe, with a rope wedgie sole. I had dressed to appeal to Maggie, not to this Hunk. I was wearing my yellow London Fog raincoat, which was boxy-shaped, so I wouldn't seem particularly threatening, and jeans, just in case she might think the raincoat was too matronly. I had washed and curled my hair, but rather than appear too flashy, I pulled it back with a tortoise-shell barrette, because everyone agrees with tortoise shell. In case she was really rich, I wore the pale-colored turtleneck that my mother-in-law gave me, so I thought I had myself covered no matter what kind of woman she was, and that we'd seem to have something in common no matter how she dressed. I had been dressing as if I were walking through a tube from my house to this bus stop and the only other person who was going to enter the tube was

Maggie and her baby stroller. But I would have dressed quite differently for a man.

I took the barrette out because it was beginning to pull the skin of my temples back so that my face seemed stretched across one of Aunt Ruth's embroidery hoops. The headache had now spread to my arms, and I needed all my strength to rock Toby and keep him asleep. When the bus finally came, it slowed and squealed to a stop like a bull elephant, sneezed open its long doors, and Debbie got on. She ran to the back of the bus as it rolled away and waved goodbye out of the fumy black window glass.

"Because horses can't throw up, silly!" she called over her shoulder as she ran away.

"You'd better go home—you look sick," the gardening neighbor said as I tilted the stroller down the curb. "Too much excitement for one day, huh?"

Because the Hunk was the first person I saw once I decided to leave my house and be really friendly, I had made a mistake and used up all my intentions on the wrong person. So when I got home I put on my nightgown and threw up all afternoon, trying to still the demands of my brain with frequent offerings from my stomach. What I threw up looked suspiciously like the stuff on the street corner that I had been standing in. All that afternoon the song I had heard playing on his car radio when he rolled down the window kept repeating and winding into Debbie's song in my mind, even when I retched: "Out came the sun . . ." I think I can see clearly now . . . And the Winky Dinky spider was sitting on the spout, grinning and sunning himself. Now, one of the really bad things about these headaches is the constant repetition of a melody over and over in my head like a record skipping. Or it is as if my thoughts, which usually come one at a time, turning slowly across a lighted radio dial, suddenly come on at once. I hear all the static, songs, outside noises, and voices, along with the regular thoughts that keep coming, because I'm still hurtling through time with the rest of the world, even though I've fallen on the conveyor belt instead of standing at attention.

The spider crawled back into the spout, and slowly the pain faded, throbbed away. Toby was still asleep. I always make a resolution of some sort when I'm finished throwing up that I'll improve something in my world because I worry so much about things when I'm sick. I keep believing that if I fix everything up, someday I won't have anything to get sick about any more. Usually I clean up the bathroom, because it's the first thing I see clearly when the headache ends and my vision opens up again.

Things looked a little different this time, however, and for the first time in a long time I looked down at myself for something to improve instead of bothering with the room. I wiped my mouth off and I swore I'd get rid of the faded, grayed nightgown I was wearing and get something new to wear, something different—softer. But I didn't want to throw this old one away, because it was the first thing I'd worn after I'd seen him, and like a kid, I thought my life had changed. This was the first time I'd had the feeling of actually longing for someone since my honeymoon. Really, since before I got married, because I was sick on my honeymoon. This new feeling that had broken in seemed like sure-fire proof that I was no longer frigid. Since I would have pressed the nightgown in a diary if I kept one, it was natural to think of making a quilt with a square of this flannel for the keystone. So for the next two hours I forgot about the bus stop and cut out squares from the things I wanted to get rid of from the present, like old sheets and house clothes, and things I wanted to remember from the past: a square from the old plaid babushka, a piece of my high-school uniform, and some squares from my wedding underwear.

At this point I was telling myself that I was celebrating the return of old feelings, and never mind what had been the instrument, and forget those hard forearms under the blue rolled-up sleeves and that giant lunar underwater watch that I'm sure glows in the dark. The idea of making something, an actual object like a quilt, out of this new feeling of longing was as satisfying as making a list of everything, absolutely everything, I wanted from the Alden's catalogue, and then I wouldn't want it so much any more. Also, I already knew that the only thing which will relieve loneliness, short of companionship, is routine. And now here was a comforting routine: lay the index card down, draw around it, cut out the fabric, pin it to the next square. Lay the index card down . . . this is how Aunt Ruth lived her whole life, I'm sure, each day a simple, square index card, filed away when finished, under the month, then the year, then the decade. Never any variation, any change, no surprises, never anything new. She had discipline, all right; day by day, she'd always do the same thing. Take any day . . .

Take Mondays, for example. On Monday, sure as the sun would come up, she'd be outside by eight o'clock in the morning, if it was below freezing and not raining, to hang her clothes. And let me tell you, there'd never, ever be any variation in how she'd hang them, either. She always separated the clothes: first, the darks from the whites, the silks from the cottons, into soft piles fragrant with the week just passed. Then she plunged the whites into hotter water than her hands could stand, stirring the biting bleach down into them with a broomstick handle. The washing machine would pound the underwear rhythmically against the bedsheets and the dish towels, and after they were rinsed and renewed and floating gently in cold water, it was my job to lift the clothes out and warily stick them by their lippy edges onto the turning hard-rubber rollers of the wringer. I was supposed to maintain an unbroken chain of wet clothes going through, to hook a sock on to a washrag on to a giant long pillowcase puffing up like ravioli with the water, because that way I could keep my fingers on the clothes and away from the rollers.

One by one the pieces were added to the wet chain rolling upward, squeezing, splashing water down my arm. If I were to let an unconnected knee sock slip out of line, it would suddenly start flapping round and round, and the wringer would scream to a stop, jammed. Once I tried to reach in for a sock before it started to go around and that was how I got my whole arm, up to the elbow, crushed by the rollers. My arm was so skinny that it didn't really hurt any more than an Indian brush burn, but Aunt Ruth got so upset that she hit me with the empty laundry basket before she loosened the rollers and freed my arm. She sat down on a pile of the darks to catch her breath, and said, "Keep it up—you'll give me a heart attack." Then she picked up the basket, and the washing continued.

Once the clothes were all squeezed out, she would carry the heavy peach basket lined with tomato-patterned oilcloth up the cellar stairs and out into the sunshine to hang them while I got dressed for school. I could watch her from my bedroom window as I dressed, as the towels went up, one by one, labels facing in, fancy side facing the neighbors. She always hung my undershirts discreetly at the end of the line, all facing sideways, phlegmatic next to her boisterous melon-size bras. She'd bleach and bleach and mend her big white underpants and then hang them in the sun to whiten like cotton fossils, and as I'd wave goodbye on the sidewalk, I'd see her struggling to get the long, gray clothes props stabbed into the lines at just the right angle—a lone Iwo Jima figure against the chicken coops and garbage cans, making the lines into triangles and the sheets into sails, masted before the helpful wind. Each week when I came home from school at three-thirty, all the clothes would be picked and she'd be at the kitchen table, folding them, folding, endlessly folding. Her big hands were of the same texture as one of the clean dish towels she would smooth first into a square and then into a smaller square, and when she had a tall stack, she would run her hand along its edges like a banker counting the day's receipts.

"The only compliment my mother ever gave me in my life was that when I folded clothes they always looked like they were ironed," she said, and that was that—every Monday the scene repeated itself and another index card was filed away.

For me, however, in this neighborhood, every day was incredibly different from the one that came before. I had expected to be talking to our new redheaded neighbor today, for example, and who would have guessed that instead I'd be crawling around on the bedroom floor looking for the pincushion and making a quilt of my own? I didn't see if he was wearing a wedding ring or not, because I really didn't believe I'd ever try to fool around with him, or with anyone back then. The second Great Truth of our marriage, in fact, the Golden Umbrella, was that we were a special couple, ours was a special love. We were different from other people. Other people fooled around, we didn't.

However, my stainless-steel corollary was that I was a "bad

seed," that I could be happy only with "forbidden fruit." I picked up this theory while reading a book called *Strange Fruit* that Aunt Ruth got from the book drop and kept hidden behind the atlas. All my important conceptions of the world were formed from the few books that were in her library. "The pear shape is the saddest thing in life for some of us," from a ladies' grooming and dressmaking book; "The greatest happiness in the world is simultaneous orgasm," from *Sex Life in Marriage*; and "If a woman stimulates herself, sensation will never mature to the vagina and she will never be able to experience the adult joy of orgasm during intercourse," from *The Illustrated Encyclopedia of Sex*. I, of course, turned out to be pear-shaped and completely frigid in married sex, having frozen myself forever to a heart-thumping but immature location of joy from the unfortunate reading of *Fanny Hill*. The great pleasure I got from reading these forbidden fruits convinced me of the truth of the other statements.

But this new quilt was already starting to change my life, I could feel it, or maybe what I could feel was the pincushion sticking me in the knee. The thing is like a Viking war wheel, because it's full of straight pins that have gotten lost inside, and the only way you can find them is to knead the thing with your fingers until one sticks you, and then you pull it out. Which reminds me of the war movie I once saw in which a lady spy, called "Pockets," because of the way her breasts filled out the army fatigues, was hiding from the Nazis in a wooden wagon filled with straw. They were approaching the dark border crossing when a German guard called, "Halt!"

"Hi, Mommy, I'm home!"

And you knew she was in there, somewhere under the straw, a plump mother-type who held all the important secrets on her person.

"What are you doing?"

So the Nazi, just to be sure there was nothing amiss, poked his bayonet through the sides of the wagon, there . . . there . . . there!

I pulled a straight pin out of my knee and stood up.

"Mom, I need some help! Please come outside, and help!"

The gardening neighbor wasn't the only person who could play outside. I checked on Toby and then went to find Debbie. All summer she had been asking for help to learn to somersault. I'd watched her from the window the last couple of times as she knelt down, placed her hands flat on the ground in front of her, stood up, and then walked toward her hands until her back was arched. Then she would wait and look at the upside-down world framed by her arms and call to me for help. She wanted me to push her over but I thought she should learn to do it by herself. A third Great Truth that Jack and I share, about which there is no disagreement, is that we are going to raise our kids better than we were raised. For me this means giving Debbie a sense of self that will keep her from needing to sniff under her dress just to see if she's still alive, and it means not lying to her about things.

She waited for me each day after school and kept calling out, "Mom! I need help!" She tried riding her bicycle without the training wheels, and when she fell she gave up and said she'd rather walk. Then she tried roller skating on the small slope of the driveway, and when she ran into the garage doors trying to stop, she again went back to simple walking. She would even have given up her somersault attempts if she hadn't inadvertently discovered the wonder of seeing the world upside down. I remember how for me the wonder at the disorientation could quickly turn to the fear of being frozen forever in a half-completed circle, with the axis of my brain and neck locked and the entry back into familiarity forever lost. So I didn't somersault much as a kid.

I remember my last bicycle ride, when I was following my friend Mary Lou through the summer-morning back roads near her house and pretending it was my own neighborhood. Her blond pony tail had disappeared over the crest of another hill, and I was still trying to pump to the top of it. When I made it, I waited for my breath to stop hurting and watched with longing as she blurred brightly down the steep road ahead—she seemed to have no fear of falling at all. Since I was embarrassed to walk my bike down the hill, I started on the descent by gripping the handlebars hard, and as the speed picked up I knew I was nothing more than a gyroscope on an invisible string with the wheels of my bike off the road and flying a little on a scrim of air and I heard the wind screaming, "Fall, fall, fall!" past my ears, so I broke the tension by steering into a pothole. Then I remember I was upside down and I felt the bicycle chain biting into my leg and Mary Lou's pony tail brushing my cheek as she bent over me to see if I was still alive. When I opened my eyes, I saw the swaying tree branches far overhead and the sun flickering through them like a million flashbulbs going off. I could see the newspaper story. There would be a photo of me, bloody, crumpled, and the headline would scream, UNGRATEFUL CHILD TRIES TO PRETEND THIS IS HER NEIGHBORHOOD AND DIES IN THE ATTEMPT. I hate irony. "Woman Who Swore She'd Never Set Foot in Airplane Dies on First Trip." *The Reader's Digest* just loves that sort of thing—the worst one I ever read was about a man who had been completely burned in a car accident, spent thirty months getting new skin to grow, and then, pow! died in a fiery crash on the way home from the hospital.

My last roller-skating experience was the afternoon a bee flew into the neck of my polo shirt as I was rolling down a long, sloping street on one of those days when I should have been in kindergarten. When I felt it buzzing in my undershirt, I started pumping my arms up and down like a windmill to try and crush it, which acted just like the propellers on an airplane, and I picked up speed and overturned a garbage can before I crashed into the telephone pole. Richard Murphey was trying to unbutton my shorts as I lay on the concrete looking at the afternoon sun in between the TV antennas, and whenever I look up at the wires I can still feel the concrete on my back and I can distinctly hear a child's voice calling, "Mom! I need help!"

Debbie was slowly rotating on the crown of her head in the grass, still waiting for me, and when I came outside, I must have looked like an alien suspended in her view, with my feet attached to a ceiling of grass and the waters of the sky racing under my head. I had managed to somersault as a kid by closing my eyes to the sickening juxtaposition of earth and sky, of sun burning into the ground, of the grass rolling upward. So I got down on my knees beside Debbie, put my head on the ground, and brought her reddening face into focus. Then the upside-down world swayed around me and I couldn't roll myself over. Seeing Jack's face upside down is one thing, as long as I myself am upright, but turning my whole self upside down is something else entirely. I could see the grass was still wet from all the rain we'd been having and full of broken dandelion stems and long, wet worms crawling from their holes. I could sense the glinting, burning bright sun and the ants and the pillbugs and the cutworms that were fighting under my palms at the very moment I pressed my hands into their dark world. I realized that if I tried, with my thirty-pound hips, I would get started in my roll and then fall over on my side like a flaccid tire that has just lost the magic of momentum.

Instead, I stood up, brushed off my hands, and, when my vision cleared, I realized I had been looking into the round wire-rimmed glasses that shone like twin suns on Maggie's long face.

"It's the lady! The lady!" Debbie said, upside down, with her small lower jaw protruding.

"I'm no lady, I'm Riva's mother," she laughed, and then, "How about coming over for some coffee?" she asked me.

Behind her glasses, I could see that there was a black, tiny, pie-shaped wedge in the green of the iris of her eye.

"The neighbor ladies tell me you're the friendliest person here." She smiled. She passed the compliment over as if she were handing me a sticky butter knife, blade first. I accepted.

"Oh, I guess it's just because I'm a good listener. Or something . . . Let me just go inside and get a few things, and we could come over for a while," I said, and I ran in to wake up Toby, and pick up the quilt squares from the floor. I decided to bring them so I'd have something to talk about, and I stuffed the squares into the back of Toby's stroller, stuffed him into the front, and followed Debbie, who was humping along on a giant plastic inchworm that rose and fell, rose and fell, along the sidewalk. We all followed Maggie down the street to her house, and I didn't care if I'd be gone when Jack called to give me his motel phone number—such is the strength of loneliness. Maggie was walking in longer-than-normal strides and carrying an armload of wildflowers.

Suburban life in the afternoon can be quite colorful and emblematic, I thought, squinting into the late sun, as we walked in parade formation. She was wearing a long red-and-gold paisley peasant dress, and she must have gathered up the flowers from the field behind our houses, where I've never gone because the path that snakes through it after the sidewalk ends is littered with beer cans and it has been said that one night a woman was raped there. In the daytime, you would most certainly get a cut and then lockjaw from such a field, at the very least.

Maggie's big house was one of the last outposts before the wildflower field, and when she pushed open her coffin-shiny but now dog-scratched front door with her bare foot, it looked to me as if the field had already grown up and into her house. I parked the stroller in the big crowded entry next to a carton full of rubber boots and mittens, an unpainted milk can with umbrellas, and a long bent tube, several balls, ballet slippers, and a tennis shoe. I dropped my bag full of quilt squares there and decided it would be safe enough to let Toby crawl around, rather than hold him on my lap, as I would have done if the Avon Lady had invited me into one of her polished rooms.

"Let me just get these into water. I'll be right back . . . come on in . . ." she said, as she carefully and, I thought, daintily followed a trail only she could see through the cluttered living room and around the corner. The white walls of the room were covered with gigantic pale art prints in thin silver frames, and then, in contrast, there were tiny dark oil paintings in large, ornate, matted frames, and shelves and shelves of books making dark leather patterns on the remaining wall space. They were stacked together so massively they seemed to form an impenetrable wall. A sculpture of what looked like a kidney with a fist breaking through the top held down a leaning pile of magazines that were scrolled open, and Toby was crawling dangerously close to an ashtray brimming with pipe stems, which I pushed out of his way. Long, hanging plants curtained the windows, and a mobile of half-chewed straw birds tilted slightly in the breeze from the opened door, sending lazy bird shadows skimming across the blue shag carpet. A big gray cat watched for a while as the phantom wings dipped up and down across the carpet and then went back to chewing the end of a weed he had pulled out of a slender jug full of nodding field grass that was leaning close to a dimly breathing, shadowing fire in the brick fireplace. Toby began pressing down the brass pedals of a baby grand that stood in a dusty pool of sunlight, letting each one of them pop up with a satisfying thunk, when Maggie suddenly flew in from the kitchen and scooped him up and away from the piano before I had a chance to look at much else in the room.

"It's the only thing I care about," she said somewhat sheepishly, carrying him toward the kitchen. "I live in mortal terror that it'll get broken."

I realized that it was time, getting past time, for me to say something, but I was stunned by several things at once: by the way that the room looked, certainly different from any other house in this development, and by the way that Maggie came running in to shield the piano in spite of all the debris and mess in the living room, which had given me the impression she didn't care particularly if anything got rumpled or touched, which was why I let Toby free in the first place. But, most especially, I was fascinated by the fact that she didn't give the traditional clenched-teeth warning to a visiting mother and child: "I'm just afraid he'll hurt himself." I mean, I'd learned nearly perfectly all the oblique, invisible dishonesties with which people navigate when they are sailing along charted social courses, and so for a second I got the feeling that the wind was changing direction and that we were going to be coming about.

"I'm sorry" was all I could think of to say.

I followed Maggie and Toby into the kitchen, beyond which I could see into the game room, where Debbie was bouncing in the bean-bag chair, next to a moving blanket stretched between two chairs. Kids of different sizes were crawling around under a Day-Glo-pink cartoon that was pulsing benignly out of a giant TV screen shaped like a four-foot curved spoon above their heads. It seemed as if all the kids, warmth, and sunlight of the neighborhood had puddled down into this brimming house at the end of the street, leaving my small gray house looking as empty and abandoned as a barnacle on a dock piling after the tide has gone out.

My eyes were eating at all the incongruities, all the broken rules that Maggie had committed in her house. It was dirty, of course, so dirty that Aunt Ruth would certainly think Maggie had sold her soul to the devil and this mess was her punishment; Jack would think she was hopeless, lower-class, and squalid to let a pile of cornflakes drift underneath her kitchen table, and the other neighbors must think of her as a blight to the street and that she would deserve it if she got murdered. If that happened, the reporters and police would take one long look at a house like this and then search it for drugs. *Better Homes and Gardens* would use her kitchen for a "before" shot.

I knew that there was going to be trouble when I saw Aunt Ruth come in by the back door and start poking around the counters behind Maggie's back. The kitchen walls were covered with black-and-white-striped Con-Tact paper that she had pasted, going first one way and then the other, all over her cabinet doors, upside down, sideways, tilted, with little chrome handles popping up at regular intervals. The field flowers were already in a Mason jar, which was sitting in a circle of water on the kitchen table. The water was seeping into the opened pages of a book, *Give Your Child a Superior Mind*, face down on the table beside the jar. I watched her open a door in the maze and take out two mugs, and when she closed it, I couldn't find the door again.

I sat down in the chair closest to the door, as a good guest would, and almost by design my eye went to the jug of flowers on the table, rather than where I knew it should go: following Aunt Ruth in her dirt-finding tour of the room. The yellows and oranges in the jar were very artistically arranged, even though I knew she had only had time to jam them in before Toby started thunking the piano pedals. The gentle colors in the flowers led my eye quite naturally up to the wall by the stove, where a big fabric collage full of similar colors filled the entire wall between the stove and the window. Scraps of fabric were formed into the shape of a sunburst rising out of two black-and-white cubes that could be dice, and the whole thing was framed in barbed wire. The words ESS IS ESS were spelled out in matchsticks and elbow macaroni. Out the window as a clever accessory was the real sun, and on the other side, in front of the stove, Maggie held a match over the burner until the flame whoomped out like a red-orange chrysanthemum, with enough force to send the fringes of the fabric dice waving gently.

Meanwhile, Aunt Ruth was ignoring the art and trying to inspect this strange kitchen I had brought her into. She felt in vain for the handles of the cabinets so she could look inside; abashed, she followed the baseboard back to the corner where the kitty litter, the garbage can, and the diaper pail had spread enough wet and dry items of a strong enough smell all over the floor so that she'd be busy sniffing and scratching there for quite a while.

"Tell me what you're doing with all that fabric," Maggie said. I watched her fill a glass dome with coffee beans and then turn it on. They jumped, and were gone into a fragrant brown haze that spread throughout the room. I wanted to stay here a while in this messy but cozy kitchen, regardless of Aunt Ruth's mounting frenzy.

"I'm making a quilt," I told her. She was listening, I suppose, while she measured the coffee into a glass tube and fitted it on top of another glass bulb full of water. Then she put it on the stove and set a timer for five minutes and sat down across from me at the table.

Now, I can't ever seem to make a good first impression, and I have several theories why this is so, since it happens so often. On the one hand, I sometimes picture myself as one of those books Debbie has where you can change a character's face by turning just the top third of the page, or change the body, or just the shoes, for a great variety of possible characters; so that while I sat across the table from Maggie for the first time, I could feel myself flipping through the several faces and poses I had acquired as protection over the years and discarding them one after the other as inappropriate. The mild, alert eyes of the respectful child; the imaginative, helpful look of the cheerful wife; the soft yet firm smile of the loving mother; the distant yet discerning poke and peer of the well-off shopper in the market; the slightly troubled would-be mental patient, disarmingly soft around the edges, yet stable in the center—all these faces I dismissed as I sat there. A slight twitching in my mouth was probably the only thing giving away my confusion. Because I got married when I was eighteen and then moved away from home, it had been five years since I had tried to make friends with someone my own age, and in that time they had all gone away to college and dormitories, revolted on TV, dropped out and been to Europe, leaving behind wistful songs about San Francisco and Boston that I listened to while I stayed home, saved coupons, and raised our two babies. Jack had gone to Vietnam without a fuss and had come back without a scratch, and when face to face with someone my own age, I don't know whether to feel superior or inferior. You could say I had a head start, you could say I had a lot of catching up to do. In any event, I certainly felt different from the rest of the people my own age, as usual. I don't want to complain, but I should have gone to kindergarten, because while I was home alone, I found a collection of dirty comic books in the milk box on our next-door neighbor's stoop. The first word I taught myself to read was "aaaaaah," and I thought "come" was misspelled in *Dick and Jane* until third grade.

Which brings up the other problem, that of too much solitude. After all the hours and months of being alone, I felt as alien sitting in that dusty, sunny kitchen with another human being as if I were a giant squid, up from the deep, dripping all over her floor. While the timer was ticking, Maggie said, "I've always loved quilts. I consider them a primary expression of woman's oppression. Those pioneer ladies were trying to tell us something, don't you think?"

I thought for a second, another second, and then, just like on *The $64,000 Queston*, I was too late: a mechanical "Time's up!" broke in, with a click click, then a long, low buzz from the ticking dial and a cheery ping. On this cue, two of the invisible kids in the game room started fighting and the blanket tent collapsed. Toby looked up from the floor, startled, his mouth full of cornflakes. "I never thought about it that way," I said over the noise and at her back as she jumped up and went to the stove.

Now, my stainless-steel rule for social discourse is that nobody ever wants to hear what you have to say. They really only want you to say something, anything, so they can get on with their next thought. I've never known it to fail, and once you get over the idealistic hurt, this rule can be very helpful. You talk anyway, of course, because people expect you to say something; the trick is to learn the right pacing, so you neither say too little and sound unfriendly or stupid, nor too much and sound, at best, boring and, at worst, crazy. Using this rule of thumb, I finished my comment on quilts by saying to Maggie's back, "My aunt made me a really beautiful one before she died. I'll have to go back and see what she might have been trying to say to me."

I could see that the oblique compliment I'd just given Maggie's taste and judgment had registered, because when she turned around, holding the steaming coffee maker over Toby's curly head, I read on her face what seemed to be a small smile buried in the freckles. Her hands were freckled, too. Freckles always remind me of the pressed ham I used to have every day for lunch if Aunt Ruth was working, so freckles always mean security for me. One freckled slice of ham on the softest white bread in the world.

Aunt Ruth was soft and padded like the white bread, with serious muscle so far below the surface she looked indestructible. When she ironed in the evening for one of the two or three families on the block, her upper arm, thick and white as a padded tailor's ham, swung back and forth, back and forth, over the ironing board. Her giant vaccination stood out against her skin like a slice of sausage. Each generation the vaccination gets smaller, I've noticed, like ethnic pride, the value of the dollar, or the worth of the person. I have my dime to Aunt Ruth's half dollar, and Debbie has only a machine-made dot that you have to take on faith, like credit-card money. Aunt Ruth would put one of her own sheets on the ironing board before she started a night's work, so that when she was finished she'd have ironed sheets just as if she'd had her own servant, too. With her head bent down as she worked, her several chins were piled neatly one on top of the other like thick plates from the diner.

Maggie, on the other hand, was very bony—her hands were the kind that remind you of your own mortality—they weren't memorable for the flesh stretched across, or for her nails, or for the three or four rings she was wearing, but rather for the way they looked like skeletal claws when she picked up the bone handle of the coffee maker. Her knuckles were oversized and raw. The only other time I'd seen knuckles that exposed was on soup bones.

"What kind of coffee maker is that?" I asked.

"Ah, it extracts the coffee," she explained. "If you're a coffee freak, like me, it's really worth the trouble. It gives you essence of coffee." While speaking, she began to pour the liquid into the mugs, making it arch into two silky quilted brown parentheses, one for her, one for me, gathering us up to the table and enclosing my unspoken thought (But I never drink coffee).

I took it black, I said, because she made it sound so good I wanted to try it straight. I have always avoided it, since Aunt Ruth lived on stale coffee and cigarettes while she worked her 5,000-piece jigsaw puzzles, and since I wasn't her real child, I swore to be as different from her as possible; and anyway, I had to keep drinking tea to get the Salada tea bags with their street-mail fortunes. My all-time favorite one was "When logic and intuition agree, you are always right."

Right now, for example, my intuition about Maggie was that she was dangerous in some way—I could feel it in the air around us—she was giving off light but no warmth. She seemed like the kind of person who would tear the world apart to find something she wanted, the type who peels a banana for just one bite, or who opens cookies in the market and leaves them there on the shelf. My instinct was to protect myself from her, which I did by asking her questions about herself, even though, as these things usually balance out, the one invited over for coffee gets to do a little more of the talking, since she is the company. But as my aunt used to say, beggars can't be choosers, and if I didn't make a good impression on Maggie, all that was left for me was the gardening neighbor.

"How many pets do you have here?" I asked.

She stopped sipping her scalding-hot coffee to think. "Last count, two kittens left from Nemesis's litter; then there's Harvey Wallbanger, whom you see in that far corner with only one good ear; then there's Hibachi, the fat cat; and Amanda's gerbils—when they run on their wheel, they turn her crib mobile and she's quiet for hours. Then there are the outside cats, and Hyacinth, the white mouse, which we hardly ever see any more now that Riva let him loose, but I keep this for him . . ." and she reached into the maze and flipped out a bread-box drawer, the kind I've always wanted to have, and then slammed it back, but not before Aunt Ruth looked up and tried to find where the bread drawer had disappeared to. "He gets in through our bedroom wall and that's his own food drawer. Last but not least is my saluki, Samantha, who's around here somewhere. My mother sent her to me as a reward for finally graduating."

College—of course, she had gone to college. I knew that already, by the way she had been dressed at the bus stop when I first saw her. I'm rarely wrong about these things. The baby she was pushing was named Amanda Maggie Mae, and she was nearly two and napping upstairs at the moment, in a hammock. I didn't tell her about the gardening neighbor's cat, which strangled by falling through the web of the hammock—why upset her?

Perhaps it was the incongruities that the paintings and the prints on the living-room wall were giving out that were bothering me. Logic says that two different kinds of taste would seem to be having a war there. There was an immense difference between the giant swirly pieces framed in silver that looked like they belonged in a Las Vegas hotel room and the careful small oils that looked as if they belonged in a museum. I believe that paintings are the windows to the soul of the person who lives in the house: look into them and you will see depths, or shallows, troubles, dreams; yet if there was a painting war on, I wanted Maggie to know I was on her side.

"I just love your prints," I told her, although I was beginning to think that Maggie might be too odd a person to have as a friend. Who needs a friend, really? Maybe solitude is an acquired taste, like anchovies, or soft cheese. Maybe she really is as bad as the gardening neighbor hints.

She paused over her mug as if she was trying to focus on something. "Which prints?"

I pointed to one of the biggest in the living room, a yellowish, greenish swirl with what looked like red beach balls bouncing near the top of it.

"Oh! *Those*. My husband was friendly with Le Roy Neiman in college and so we keep them around just in case he honors us with one of his unexpected visits that last for a week. They're really not my taste—that's Chuck for you."

"Chuck? Did you say Chuck?"

"Sure, Chuck, my husband, Chuck. Short for Charles Richard Matheson IV; little Dicky, aptly named. Do you know him from somewhere?"

Auspicious coincidences are also a form of street mail, I was thinking. God must want me to meet the Hunk, because here I am in his own kitchen. I was a little overawed by fate.

"Hey, wait a minute, you know who he is, I bet. He told me he saw a short lady at the bus stop this afternoon standing in the rain, with a baby in a blue stroller. It must have been you and . . . what's your baby's name again?" She slapped her knee and had a private laugh, with a "humph" in it. "What we both want to know," she said, "is how did you manage to stand in those stinko ginkgo berries all that time? I nearly asphyxiated! And Chuck said that when he rolled the window down, he nearly reeled over backward from the stench! I think he might have gotten a funny impression of you—he said you looked so stoic standing there."

At least I wasn't invisible.

"He got it all screwed up, of course. I told him before he left for work today that she was on alternate, but his head is some place else. Riva's his, not mine—she's his six-year-old from a rotten five-year marriage. Chuck has custody of her and I try to adjust."

"Adjust?"

"To another kid around here, when sometimes I want to be the only child. To the ghost of his ex-wife, who haunts me through Riva . . ."

"Is she dead?"

"I wish she was. God, no, she's a lawyer—brilliant, of course. Gorgeous, ditto—she's a D.A. in Boston, Barbara Matheson—she kept his name, can you believe that?" She calls Riva between cases, giving me just enough time to paste the kid back together before she calls again. It's a no-win thing we've got going here, and it's anybody's guess how long I'm going to put up with it. I don't know what your politics are, but I really have a hard time condoning that woman's neglect."

My politics are unspeakable, so I thought it better not to mention them and instead to listen to Maggie, who was beginning to make me feel superior as she listed the ills of her particular situation. First conversations are usually spent reviewing one's assets and liabilities, I've found. When it comes to politics, however, I've always been in the wrong place at the wrong time, so that I can never seem to play the right games. You know the one about where were you when Kennedy got shot? And everybody says, "In the classroom. I looked up at the clock on the wall and the teacher made us bow our heads . . ." Well, I can't tell anyone where I was because I had skipped classes, playing hooky for the first and last time in my life, and I was at a lonely ice-cream stand in the country long after the weather had turned too cold for ice cream. I was in the car of the really disreputable older brother of a neighborhood kid who was known for his ability to lie while swearing on the cross. I was vaguely considering, you know, sex or something, but first I was going to make sure I got some ice cream, and then, while I was eating, decide exactly what I was going to do. Don't get me wrong—I was still what you would call a "good girl," I mean, I had never gone all the way. I liked to tease, however, and I think I had hoped to get myself on a path of no return with this older brother of the liar, because I was getting so nervous with the constant strain of preserving my saintly virginity that I couldn't stand the pressure. I hate waiting. At least if he forced me, it wouldn't be my fault. But when we pulled up to the ice-cream place, the radio was beeping news bulletins, and the girl inside was crying, pressing her forehead against the wire screen so that her skin was waffled through to our side of the grille. There's a very thin line between virtue and being bad, as thin as the grate in the confessional through which you squeeze your sins. I had thought I would just confess a sin against the sixth commandment of actual lust the next time I went on Saturday, instead of against the mere ninth commandment of wishful thinking. To order up something special, rather than my usual. So I have a hard time believing that innocence was lost for us all that day. For me, it was preserved, and the older brother became a Jesuit on the promptings of that one experience. So you see, it was an auspicious day for both of us, because I was still a virgin when I met Jack and I think he liked that best about me, and now that it's gone, he's not all that thrilled with me. "It's never the same after the factory seal is broken," he jokes. But the day that Kennedy got shot, Aunt Ruth thought I was in school, and all my friends, including Richard Murphey, my boyfriend, thought I was sick at home.

I've always, always, had a boyfriend. I'm not ugly, and except for Mary Anne Garibaldi and her stupid sausage curls, I was nearly the prettiest girl in my class, maybe. I don't know—I'm on the inside—you can't tell on Halloween whether you're wearing the Snow White or the Wicked Witch mask unless you look in a mirror—life is no different. I've always had a boyfriend, except for 1968, when Jack was in Vietnam, and then I was totally celibate, a condition which contributed to my current problem, I think. A terribly thick, yet resilient crust has formed over me since that year, very much like the crust on pudding. It's nice and soft, but you have to break through it to get to the pudding—an act of violence neither Jack nor I seem willing to perform. In 1968, when the whole world was watching, what do you think *I* was watching? Not the Democratic National Convention, in which history was being made in the streets, no. I was glued to the first installment of the *Hawaii Five-o* series, the movie in which McGarrett is sealed off from the world.

And I rooted for the police, anyway, as I always had been taught to do. But if I had gone away to college, away from Aunt Ruth, with people my own age to influence me, there's no telling—I might have been out in the street, getting my head knocked in, too. So let's not talk about politics.

"More coffee?"

I thought, Does she want me to stay, or should I go? Should I stick my neck out and ask for more, which is really saying I'm asking for more company; or should I be cool and distant, polite and reserved, and say, No thanks, we've got to be getting on? She seems so unconventional, surely these delicate rules don't exist for her. She's probably only steering through life with a simple bit of honesty for a rudder, pure honesty. So I stuck my neck out.

"Sure, I'd love some—it's really rich!"

But I was wrong. She jumped up and said, "Oh, it's getting late! Let me just check on Amanda—I've got to get her cleaned up before Chuck gets home. I'll just be a minute . . . here—" And she poured me some coffee, a little comma, and said, "Enjoy."

Our beginnings of friendship seemed to be progressing like one of those handcars you see in a Charlie Chaplin movie, in which one person pulls one way and the other person pulls the other way, and then the whole thing rolls forward, propelled by opposite pressures. While she was upstairs with the baby, I blew on my coffee to cool it, so I could drink it and leave as quickly as possible. Aunt Ruth was trying to slide her good thumbnail under the chrome on the stove top to get at the black paste there. She always said your thumbnail is your most important cleaning aid. My breath rippled the shiny surface of the coffee so that it sparkled blackly in the sunlight. When I looked at the shine, I allowed my eyes to glaze over into a stare so I could lose the edges of the room and fall into the white light in the blackness of the coffee. Aunt Ruth used to hit me with the whipped-out edge of the dish towel when she saw me doing that—she said I looked like a nincompoop, and she was probably right. But what she doesn't know is that I had taken one of her puzzle pieces so that she could never finish the damn thing as long as I was around. It was because of Winky Dink—I really wanted a Winky Dink.

Out of the corner of my eye I saw a quiet bit of movement in the flowers on the table. A tiny brown spider was dipping into the dappled shade behind some goldenrod, and if I didn't keep an eye on it, I knew it would drop right into my coffee. Then Maggie was back, carrying my bag of quilt squares.

"I think you'd better hold on to these—I just found Harvey Wallbanger in them. He must have thought it was some new litter. I hope he didn't mess them up too badly," she said, and handed them to me. "So tell me what your quilt is going to say."

I wanted to say, "Nothing," and just get out and go home and think about things for a while, but I swallowed that word with some of the bitter coffee and looked for the spider before answering. I felt as if it were crawling on me. Maggie poured herself some coffee, reluctantly, I thought, and sat down again. The spider had stepped onto a white fringe of Queen Anne's lace and was moving toward the purple bead in the center when she spoke again. "You know, it's funny. Chuck has been saying that I'm not going to like this neighborhood, that I'm not going to be able to get along with any of the women here because I'm half their age. He thought you were much older—he said you ladies would hate me because I don't like to clean and I can't cook worth a damn. I consider myself an artist, frankly, not a housewife. Actually, the only thing I've ever learned to cook is coffee and salad, but I don't complain —I'm afraid if I get interested in cooking I'll get so fat I'll have to sit around and eat bonbons all day after that."

Don't be so quick to condemn bonbons, I thought to myself. It takes great courage to sit and eat them. Think about it—each one is completely covered with dark uncertainty, and you don't know what's going to be inside the next one any more than you know what a new day will bring. And the lady who sits and eats them is touching that uncertainty with her sensitive tongue, tasting, biting, swallowing, whatever comes along, sight unseen. And also, don't forget that those chocolates are unique for their ability to hurt the teeth worse than anything else. So you get the cherry or instant, excruciating pain. It takes guts to risk those odds, believe me. I realized that there was no point in telling all this to Maggie. She was too interested at the moment in telling me what a unique individual she was, come here like a just-hatched nature sprite to breathe new life into this dying neighborhood.

"I admire you for doing something homey and substantial with your time," she was saying, fingering one of the fabric squares, a piece of my wedding dress, in fact.

"Well, I believe in weaving a web of mystery," I said in my enigmatic way, as I watched the spider move past the purple bead, off the flower, and then slide down a thread to the tabletop.

"But which is the mystery, you or the quilt?" She smiled.

The spider moved slowly across the table.

"Oh, God! I forgot to take something out of the freezer for dinner!" she said, and jumped up from the table again.

The spider crawled over the rim of her mug and disappeared. I waited until she sat down, and then I watched her drink her coffee before I got up to leave. I gathered up my fabric squares and kids, and grabbed Aunt Ruth, who was trying with both hands to unstick the flour canister from the countertop by rocking it sharply back and forth, but it was glued there by inches of grease and peanut butter.

"It's no use," I told her, and we all went home.

The next day, I decided to try and wipe Maggie's cat's mess off the squares I could save and arrange them on the kitchen floor in pretty piles of color because I've always liked stacking up my supplies more than actually making something of them. Toby was in his tilted baby seat on the kitchen table, making faces out the window at the empty porch, when I heard the knocking. At first I thought he might be rocking off the table, but when I looked up, he was still smiling out the window. I looked around the kitchen—the only other thing in the room where the knocking could be coming from was the cardboard box with Aunt Ruth's quilt in it that I had dragged into the kitchen to do something with once I'd finished cleaning up my own quilt squares. There was knocking again, and I looked over into the box, lifting up the quilt warily, in case there was a mouse in there knocking around in the wooden canisters I was going to throw away.

"Allo . . . allo! . . . anybody home?"

God, it was someone at the back door—a sound that was still so alien to me that it nearly scared me, and worse, I'd just gotten everything set up for a nice afternoon of solitude. I'd put the water on to boil for spaghetti.

"Watcha doin'?" Maggie asked rhetorically as she pulled her red wagon over to the back steps to unload it. She had packed Amanda and a large cardboard box marked *Syringes 100 Count* onto it, and for an insane second I pictured her forcing me into a life of heroin addiction that very afternoon. Then, in a simple, manic gesture, before I could say "Come in" or "Go away," she reached down and pulled up Amanda and stood her on the porch. She gave her a little push forward, identical to the gesture Debbie uses for Baby-Talks-a-Lot by pulling her string so she performs. I knew, before they came in the back door, that this was going to be Baby-Wrecks. I could picture it: my house will belong to this baby—she will have won it by the law that says the weak and the helpless come first. Every wall outlet and every wire, every pot I put on the stove, and every stair step, every small thing on the floor, from bugs to dust to paper clips, will be hers. All the furniture I keep highly polished will be hers for the fingerprinting, and I'll have to put away all my knickknacks and books, and ashtrays. She will claim my magazines, simply by placing one fat wet palm in the middle of a page, making a fist, and then bringing the wadded page up to her slobbering mouth. And the only thing I can say, as I run before her gathering up the china cup of strawflowers, is "I'm just afraid she'll hurt herself, that's all."

"Uh—hi . . . has Amanda had the flu yet?" I asked Maggie, who was still struggling with the carton. Amanda was pulling out the cascade of green strings and buds from the little potted plant that had finally started growing for my gardening neighbor.

"What? No . . . yes . . . who knows . . . that's for Chuck to worry about—he's the doctor—there! This sucky little thing is heavy!" The playpen that she finally pulled from the box was suddenly exposed, pristine in its welcome, simple beauty—a small square of pine on wheels with a partially chewed mattress. Amanda screamed and threw down the plant when she saw it, but no matter.

"Little bitch . . . come on, sweetie . . . you know Mommy has lots of *work* to do today . . . ow! Make no mind of Amanda . . . stop that! Amanda's having a little sugar reaction . . . there!" And she was trapped; screaming, with strings from the plant and hairs from her mother in each fist, but trapped. "Where can we put her? Do you have a TV? Wait, I've got it—you've got another kid, too, right? At the bus stop, little Doodie—"

"—Debbie."

"—Debbie told me that you're dying for someone to play with yours. Isn't that just great! Maybe we could switch off on some baby-sitting sometime—I'm going stir-crazy down there cooped up all day—how about you? Is that your kid in the window? What's that you've got him in?"

"Why don't you come in . . ."

"Isn't he the cutest thing today! What's wrong with his feet?"

"Nothing—yet. Jack—my husband—just thinks the brace would be good insurance for later. Then, he says, Toby's legs have no choice but to grow straight."

"What is your husband, some kind of macho-nut?"

"He's a salesman," I began automatically. "What do you mean?"

"And you must be a Mrs. Macho-nut to go along with such a harebrained idea! *God*'ll grow them straight! Whew! Don't ever let Chuck see that—he'd have you arrested, he's got such a soft heart . . . among other things. It's a good thing your husband didn't ever hear what the gypsies did to kids . . ."

"What?"

"You really want to know? Promise you won't tell your Attila-the-Husband?"

"What?"

"Hey, what's all that steam coming from your kitchen?"

Now, nobody on earth, I guarantee, would ever admit that she was making a pot of spaghetti to eat alone in the middle of the afternoon. "Oh! I'm just humidifying the kitchen, where I'm working. I think I'm coming down with the flu."

"Well, let's put Amanda in there, since that's the healthiest place. Come on, sweetstuff . . . we're going for a little ride. Look at this kitchen! So neat and clean. What else do you do all day besides clean? Ah . . . you're still working on that quilt—is that how you're doing it—making little piles first? *Wait* just one little minute! What's this?" And she had Aunt Ruth's quilt out of the box faster than I could turn off the spaghetti water. "Isn't this gorgeous! Did *you* do this incredible thing? And where did you ever come by all this talent?"

I told you, no one ever listens to what you say. Not only did she forget Toby's very existence from one day to the next, but she also forgot our whole conversation about Aunt Ruth's quilt yesterday, just as she forgot to finish the story of what the gypsies do. Now I'm going to have to seem like a compulsive nitpicker if I remind her about any of this, rather than a devil-may-care conversationalist who can float and toss on any whims. Or, since there's no way for her to know any differently, I could take credit and say that I'm the artist—I made the quilt. But I can't lie—I'm much too superstitious, or too Catholic.

"My Aunt Ruth made it for me."

"Wow! It's so ugly it's actually beautiful, you know. It forces your eyes back to it each time they try to get away—happily horrid, don't you think?"

"I don't think . . ."

"I love playing with the parameters of an artistic construct," she said, crouching in front of the box of things I wasn't sure of, like the plastic placemats with the quilted edges where food always gets caught, the naked-lady stirrers that Jack brought back from Idaho, the wooden canisters shaped like tree stumps. "What art does to the eye—how it controls the viewer—you know what I mean? I mean, as ugly as this quilt is, it forces me to look at it. But once I did something quite the opposite, which I considered more than revolutionary at the time. It was when I was in San Juan—"

"You were in San Juan? That's a coincidence! When? We were there on our honeymoon!"

"Well, my trip was no honeymoon, I can tell you that—I'd just gotten out of jail."

"Jail? In Puerto Rico?"

"And I had so little to work with in the way of materials, you know . . . and I was feeling pretty alienated, so I created my Revolutionary Sculpture."

"Why were you in jail?"

"Political espionage, I like to say—somebody framed me—planted two lousy little grass seeds smack in the middle of my daddy's custom blue-tufted Caddy upholstery. Framed! Probably because I slept with Tom Hayden. That was when they realized that the Ugly American was also the Rich American—I'm lucky my father owns property there, or I wouldn't be here today."

"Wow . . ."

"I'll tell you wow—you tell me if you don't think this was a dynamite idea: a sculpture composed of stuff so gross you *had* to look away! You had no choice—it was a play on your conditioned responses, among other things. Do you have anything to drink?"

Of course! My first social moment in the neighborhood had come and I'd nearly missed it. "I'll make some tea."

"Tea! That's cute! . . . anyway, picture this . . ."

And while I got the mugs out and checked them for stains, and emptied the kettle all the way out to get rid of as many of the calcium flakes in the bottom as I could, she described a sculpture so horrible, so gross, so disgusting, that I'm embarrassed to repeat it, even now. Let me just say that it contained things normal people put into the garbage disposal, or flush down the toilet, all of which she said she had arranged in the steamy Puerto Rican heat, on top of what she called "the most disgusting object of all—a plastic Rubbermaid lazy Susan."

Aunt Ruth, by now, was aghast. I know she wanted to open my cabinet door and point out my nearly complete collection of Rubbermaid and Tupperware, all nested according to size, all squeaky clean, but I held her back.

"I'd do something so horrible it can't be believed, rather than settle for mediocrity," Maggie was continuing. "Take these toys, for example." She picked up Toby's pumpkin camper, my particular favorite, next to the pear cement mixer, of the whole Fruit Group of rolling toys. "This is a classic case of mediocrity—just make it good enough to get by with—don't go out on any design limbs, don't rock any boats . . ." She was holding his toy above his head now, and Toby started to cry, indignant, at about the same time that the teapot whistled. "Kids don't know any better—it's really up to us, as parents, to supply them with playthings that will stimulate their imagination, not deaden it." But she gave the camper back, anyway, and Toby hugged it in happy, maybe deadened, silence.

" 'Mediocre' literally means the middle of the mountain, and that's nowhere. Maybe that's why it's so frightening to me," she said. "I actually get an asthma attack when Riva wants to go to McDonald's and I have to sit in there waiting for her to finish a Ronald Turd and all I have to look at are colonial scenes of Independence stamped out, like in *1984*, at the factory. Don't you have any herbal tea?"

"Just Salada . . ."

"Nothing for me, then. Where was I? I'll have to bring my own—I can't drink that stuff. I have some so good it's nearly a trip in itself . . . where was I?"

"In the middle of the mountain . . ."

"Ah yes, the kaleidoscope. Here—check this out." And she reached into her big woven bag and handed me a long, intricately carved wooden tube with a wheel at one end. "It's Amanda's favorite thing in the whole world, but we'll let you see it, too, won't we, sweetie?" Amanda was curled, nearly comatose, in her playpen, chewing on the end of the mattress and twirling a reddish curl with her free hand. She continued to watch the side of the refrigerator and didn't answer when I took the toy and looked inside, as Maggie insisted I do.

"Isn't that something else?" she called to me as I entered the tube. I aimed it at Maggie first, and she broke into a brilliant Roman candle of red fuzz. Then, turning slowly around the room, I exploded my cabinets into a thousand green fragments, with the white-handled knobs dotting through them like tiny tulips. The steam from the kettle waved in gray silken scarves through a porcelain crystalline structure of stove: and dry ice in an endless frozen cave . . .

I had to have the kaleidoscope.

"Gee, that's really nice . . . hmmmm . . . neat . . . where'd you get it?"

"My mother sent it from Germany. She probably knocked on the back door of some little cottage in the Black Forest and then jewed the stooped little guy out of his last artifact. But I'm sure there's nothing like it anywhere around here. Mother searches the world for the unique . . ."

"Oh. Why is your mother in Germany?" I asked, casually putting the toy on the counter beside the tea canister.

"Well, do you want her version or her doctor's version?" Maggie asked, suddenly turning and looking out the window. I pushed the kaleidoscope just a tad more behind the canister. "She's so hateful!" Maggie was nearly whispering and twirling the tassel on the window shade as she spoke; twisting, twisting, twisting. "She has a *trinken* problem, if you get my drift." And the tassel popped off in her hand. "Great goin', Mag," she said to herself, wiping away a tear.

I shoved the toy behind the canister and said, "Say, don't worry about that."

"I can't help it—every time I have to talk about her, the same thing happens. Her boozing is what ruined our whole family—my father had to leave, he had no choice—here—what do you want me to do with this? Did you crochet this yourself? Look at this, Amanda, Mommy's crying again."

And nowhere have I read what you should do with a stranger in your own kitchen who is crying. Aunt Ruth shook her head and looked at her watch.

"Well!" I said. "How do you like the neighborhood?"

"Don't make me laugh." She sniffed, looking for something to blow her nose in. I gave her a flowered cloth napkin. "Are you out of tissues?" she asked, and then blew a long, forlorn, foggy kind of sound.

"Well, that's a long story," I began . . .

"Save it. Let me tell you—I can't be*lieve* this place! Can you?"

"Well, I thought it reminded me of a play village when I first saw it," I began, artistically enough.

"Damn right—Plasticville, U.S.A. I'm convinced this place is a big fake—I bet it's really a Potemkin village."

Oh boy, here come the college references. And after that comes my admission of stupidity. "What do you mean?"

"Potemkin—you know—Catherine the Great's, I guess, great lover. He was also a general, and when she wanted to ride past the peasants, she wanted everything to look hunky-dory, and he wanted to get laid, so he had these fake fronts set up, like a movie set—you know—and the peasants stood in front and waved and cheered and looked insanely happy, like in a McDonald's commercial. While their own houses were squatty and smelly and falling down behind. And she was happy and he got his rocks off. The End."

"Is that true?"

"Far as I know."

"That's fascinating!"

"Stick with me, kid, and I can teach you loads of stuff." She stood up. "We've gotta go. This obligatory friendship visit is all well and good, but it's got to end sometime, and when my stomach starts growling—I answer back. Listen, why don't you and the little gimpy kid come down to my place tomorrow? Bring your sewing project, and bring that gorgeous quilt. We'll take it apart and make something out of it." She nudged Amanda. "Come on, babe, Mommy's got to get something to eat . . . I'm sorry about your window thing . . . you really should take those shades down, anyway—they only block the sun."

And then she was gone. I turned the spaghetti water back on and walked around the empty rooms for a few minutes, touching things gingerly, now that I'd had some company. Everything felt strange. Her presence and her words were still there, and I was sensitive for a little time after she left, as if I'd just pulled a splinter out and the skin was still sore.

The next day, while I was finding clean clothes for Toby for the walk to Maggie's, I also tried to make the beds before I left, but one by one I was beginning to let my jobs go undone, so I could chase after her. I hadn't vacuumed now for a couple of days and Jack would be home the day after tomorrow. It's not that I'm any kind of neatness nut: I was actually really sloppy as a kid, my aunt says, but I think you can't deny the fact that the only way you have any hope of elegance is through cleanliness. I like to think about the whiteness of a day at the Naval Academy, or the dresses Kitty Carlisle wore in an old movie—that's elegance, totally based on being clean. Diana Vreeland's maid irons her money for her, and Jackie Onassis has her sheets changed every time she touches them. Cleaning things up is one of the few positive actions you can take against the clinging, rotting, dragging tendrils of mortality that get everything in the end, breaking everything down.

And so I left the dishes in the sink, telling myself that at least I was cleaner than Maggie, which was one of my bigger mistakes. You're supposed to try to be as good as the best, not better than the worst.

I gathered up Aunt Ruth's quilt so Maggie and I could rip it apart, and Toby, and went down the street to Maggie's, thinking that any neighbors who were watching would probably be saying I've finally fallen to my own level. And they were around, I could feel them there, partially hidden by the bushes. Glynnis said, "How's the hippie?" as I rolled Toby past her mailbox and she took her Book of the Month out. "Can you believe it—they used an ambulance to move their junk in with! What gall! I'm going to check to see if there isn't an injunction against using public property that way—what if I were going to have a heart attack and they had it loaded up with dishes! Be careful with that one," she finished, banging the mailbox shut. The gardening neighbor waved as I passed, and the Avon Lady merely watched from her window until I turned into Maggie's cluttered driveway, and then dropped her white ruffled curtain before I could see her expression.

Each time I saw her, Maggie looked different—that was one of the things that was the most fun about her. She really dressed like an artist. She wore hand-embroidered tunics over tissue-thin jeans, and dark sweaters, with hand-tooled sandals and hand-bent silver earrings. Her hair was usually loose, but the shades and tones of red changed, depending on whether she'd just put avocados, or lemons, or mayonnaise all over it for the morning.

"Don't breathe a word about this nifty staying-home routine to a soul, or I swear, they'll take it away from us! It's too fantastic to be true," she used to say on a good day. "Do you realize what I can do—how terrific I can look? I can stand on my head for hours at a time, put tea bags on my eyes, and raise my IQ while I reverse gravity. I can wear a mask, fast, cleanse my entire system—and I'll look ten years younger than the idiots who are begging to work! And you know what they look like? Crawling to the tub at the end of the day. Picking off their calluses with cruddy fingernails. They're covered with paper cuts, and guess who's going to start looking awfully good to the hubbies at a party—me! And these working women fall asleep halfway through any party, anyway. Who needs it! But keep your mouth shut, you hear?"

Now, when I brought my quilt over that particular morning, her hair was tied up in white papers and she said I was just in time to help her pack, because she was quitting, leaving, running away. She said she hated Chuck more than words could tell, and she turned so quickly from the front door back into the living room that some of the papers flew out. One fluttered past me and settled down on top of the quilt in the back of the stroller, and I wondered if Chuck would be as easy to catch if she let him go drifting free like that.

Her clothes were spread all around the room: wools, velvets, cashmeres, silks, and she was stuffing some black lace underwear and some sweaters into a gray duffel bag. "I'm not really leaving for good—I'm just gonna shake him up a little. He's got to see that he can't treat me like he treated Barbara. Now I know why she left him, and I sure got the booby prize in that contest." When the bag was full, she zipped it and rolled it across the room. "Damn him! After all the trouble I went through—" and she kicked it over to the door. "If you could just hide a few of my things at your place, he'll really worry, and I'll spend a night or two out, just for good measure. Will you do it?"

And so in a matter of a half hour I was walking back up the street past the Avon Lady's curtain and Glynnis's mailbox with two of Maggie's angels on the red wagon. They were from the church she was christened in before it was modernized, and they were life size.

"Don't worry what people say," she called from her doorstep, white curler papers fluttering like butterflies, as I started down the street. "Just think to yourself, If *I* do it, it's *done*."

The next day I was emptying the trash and trying to remember how this incredible week had begun by looking through its remnants there in the metal can. The problem with poor people, I decided, is that they are too connected with material things, details, doors closing, the other shoe falling. Perhaps it comes from a racial memory of taking care of other people's things, but poor people, peasants, always follow the bouncing ball and are perfectly fooled by magic. Maggie, on the other hand, seemed to care only about her own feelings—all the things in the world were placed here for her use—they had no being apart from that. I heard her coming down the street, singing, and I didn't look up until she was as close as her singing voice would let her get—her idiosyncrasies enabled her to keep a little extra social distance—say, the amount a large summer hat would have given you in the olden days.

"Watcha doin'?" she sang.

"You're back already?"

"Just for the season. I told him I'd go through one more season here, get my money's worth, so to speak, before this place drives me bats."

"HEY, LADIES! SHOW US YOUR COFFEE MAKERS!" she yelled, so suddenly and so loud that the lid clattered out of my hand. "You watch—one of those suckers'll come running out with a Mr. Coffee if we stand here long enough. Let's go inside and light a fire. I'm freezing."

"I brought my own tea this time," she said, settling into Jack's armchair. "Specially blended on the Colombian shores, or slopes, or whatever."

"Where's Amanda?"

"Sleeping with Chuck. Very, very kinky, but what are you gonna do? He's gonna be her mommy, he can do it better than me. We do Open Marriage, you know?"

"He fools around?" I asked, casually enough.

"You can't fool around if you have Open Marriage—that's the beauty of it. The rules are different, but they're just as strict, because this is a very touchy situation. You're both trying to screw the other while pretending to be so supportive it's nauseating. There's not supposed to be any sexual duplicity, that's all. Fucking means so little, really—just ask one of your husband's secretaries."

"Well, you know, Jack swears to me he works too hard, he's too old, and we have two kids . . ."

"And you're too cute for words. Is the water boiling yet? I've seen your little hubby flitting through the neighborhood. He's a pretty fine specimen for you to be acting so smug."

"Yes, but you don't have to open his suitcase and smell his underwear when he's had it packed in a hot climate for over a week."

"Oh, I don't think you have anything to worry about, not yet, at least. It looks like you and Jack still have some vital signs. Open Marriage is strictly Intensive Care—for the terminally bored. And usually the patients run out, and besides, who cares, right? Remember, it's style, not sincerity, we're after at this stage. Here—have a sniff of this tea— you'll admire its style after a while, I can promise that, at least."

Which is how I ended up sewing my first fabric collage of two hundred or so buttons on a dish towel until the tea wore off.

"Do what I say and you'll have a fine piece of work," she said. "You have to think big, like I'm always telling Chuck. Get beyond yourself, think into the thing you hold in your hand, feel the immenseness of it. Become one with it."

"Become a button?" It was Aunt Ruth's voice, coming out of my own mouth.

"Sure, mother-of-pearl, slipping in and out of tight holes, popping off at the worst times . . ."

"You know," I interrupted, "don't you hate it when you always have to pull the thread that goes back and forth, back and forth, back and forth, and then the button falls off; yet you can't find the right thread that will zip open the sack of rice?"

"You buy rice by the *sack*? Haven't you ever heard of Minute Rice?"

"Listen! I'll teach you how to become an artist," she said when she poured more tea. "It's the least I can do," she began. I watched her mouth. "The artist, as teacher, is everyone's parent, because only he or she bothers to think for everyone else. I'm sure Norman Mailer is my real father. He's got lots of kids he doesn't know about and my mother—well, forget her. I knew we were spiritually connected when I read his interview in *Playboy* and I wasn't afraid to die for a full hour afterward." She had slightly buck teeth, and she was very careful not to spit as she talked. I appreciated that. "I'm always afraid of death otherwise—can you *believe* it—I can't. And I sat on the grass after I read that interview and I tested myself—and it was true—for the space of that hour, I wasn't even afraid of the dude I was living with, and he was a nice rough character, I can assure you. But that's exactly what an artist does—he keeps you from being afraid of the dark for little bits of time, just like your parents used to, before they started drinking, and then, for Crissakes, I was even afraid of my own mother! But I can prove all this, lest I rave . . ." and she pulled out her sketch pad from deep within her batik bag. "I can create you, just like any parent can. Here—let me draw you. Tell me, how did you see yourself when you first moved to this Godforsaken place?"

I told her only the good stuff.

"Now, as I draw," she said, "I always lose myself in the piece—I become the vehicle, the transporter, for something greater, brighter than me. Finally, when it really gets hot, I actually feel transparent." She looked up. "Invisible tissue, once the flame of inspiration passes through . . ." She looked up again. "Then I collapse in on myself like a Chinese lantern from yesterday's garden party. There."

She handed me a sketch, and without ever having seen her, she'd drawn a picture of Aunt Ruth, in the flesh, wearing an apron with long strings, leaning on a broom, with a plaid peasant babushka on her head. I burned red with embarrassment.

"Give that back—you're not like that any more," she said, tossing it into the fireplace. "Here's what you're like now . . ."

And while Aunt Ruth darkened and burst into red flames, she drew me in the present: as a slow, grinning Gila monster watching a lone fly buzzing over my head.

There's an old trick I used to practice to hypnotize myself. It was supposed to distort real time by changing subjective time. You had to lose yourself in a color or an object and then, before you knew it, whoosh—ten minutes would fly by, unconnected to the tyranny of the clock.

It's a good way to describe the year that has intervened between that afternoon with Maggie sketching in front of the fire and last night's orgy. Above all, I want to avoid any mental picture of big numbered days being ripped off a desk calendar by an invisible hand while a few autumn leaves blow around, followed by a little bluebird that lands on the calendar to announce the arrival of spring. No, that's not how time goes. I hate the thought of it dripping away, ticking away, or being ripped out of my mother-in-law's checkbook with a flourish and a "What day is it, anyway?"

No, that's not how it goes. And for God's sake, please don't picture things physically speeding up, with the sun bouncing up, then down, up, down, like a giant yellow beach ball caught in the Time Machine, or the trees turning green and then catching fire one by one: poof, poof, poof, and then they're skeletons again. It's never, never like that, except in a nightmare.

No, I prefer to think of the past as a big scrapbook that comes to life when I open the pages, just like in the beginning of *I Remember Mama*. Obviously, the memories you put in the scrapbook shape the way you want to remember the past, rather than the exact way it really happened, but then nothing is perfect, not even the past. Memory is, after all, the street mail of the mind.

We will proceed by staring into the fire. Notice how it looks like a waterfall going the wrong way, pouring silken reds over the rocks and coals? Concentrate on the color red, which now first appears, shiny and clean, rolled out in long vinyl exercise mats in the high-school gym, where Maggie and I went every Tuesday night for yoga classes. She meditated every day, she told me, and I needed to lose some weight; she told me that, too. We were both extremely typical—she of a type of self-love, I of self-hate. Or, at the very least, self-avoidance. I don't like to be as involved with my body as exercises force you to be—I'd prefer to just work it from the conning tower of my head, rather than get down there and tussle with it hand to hand.

I had wrapped myself up with thirty or so extra pounds of nice safe fat so that Jack was never really touching me but rather my insulating covering of pudding crust. Maggie detected the fat on me no matter how I tried to camouflage it, while Jack said he thought I looked fine—no need to bother. Men want to be fooled into believing you have a decent body, I think, so their eye is easily distracted from the problem areas by a fluff of breast or a curly eyelash; but women need to compare, and it's an easy matter for them to zero in, since we're all working with the same stuff. Maggie decided to improve me, and she saw it as her mission to intervene and save my marriage from a fate worse than Open.

The first time Jack ever saw her she had tied her long, red hair up on top of her head with a pink ribbon to match the even hotter-pink leotard she wore under her long-haired coat. He acted like an idiot, kissing first her hand and then mine, joking that he was glad I'd finally brought a good-looking woman into his life. Jack thought he was being honest by telling me how much other women turned him on, but it was painful to hear this, because the small breasts and boyish hips that he liked so much now were what I'd never have again. We were both longing after my ghost, it seemed.

I wanted to drive to yoga myself the first night, but Maggie insisted: it was her treat. She had a hiking boot for driving that she kept in her old, dented Chevy, because the flat part of the brake was broken off and she had to press down on the stump of the pipe that was left. Should she have to stop suddenly, the pressure would cut right through the sole of a regular shoe. Besides, her foot kept falling off the brake, and at least the boot had some grid left on it, she said. She also said that her hands had a tendency to sweat on the steering wheel when she was nervous, and just as we were driving onto the entrance ramp of the turnpike, she said she really had to go to the bathroom.

"It's this damn leotard—it's made for a Barbie doll, not me. I'm anatomically correct, and it's not," she said, crossing her legs once, and then again, so she looked like a doctor's snake all wrapped above the boot on the brake pipe. "Let's talk about something interesting to keep my mind occupied," she said, and when we went under a highway lamp, I could see that the steering wheel was glistening wherever her hands touched it. "Did you have to get married, or something? Debbie *is* your own kid, isn't she?"

So I told her about how Jack was such an excellent salesman—he could sell anybody anything, without ever looking touched by the transaction himself. He was therefore able to sell me on the idea of quitting my job and college and getting married when I was eighteen. "Your credit is good and there's no money down," and I didn't even have to be pregnant. Now, however, after two babies, I looked ten years older than I should, but he still looked the same as he did when we got married—it's not fair! It's like the army boots he had at Officer Candidate School. He used to amaze everyone by being the first at formation every morning, starched crisp, with the miles of laces perfectly tight and tied on his spit-shined boots. Of course, what nobody knew was that he had seven pairs of boots, all specially altered by a shoemaker in town with zippers on the sides. The zippers were hidden when he stood at attention. And the worst part is that he sold every pair of boots for three times what they were worth when he got out—he's an excellent salesman. For all I know, right this very minute he could be selling the whole idea of marriage again to another eighteen-year-old while I careen down the highway at top speed with this hot-pink caduceus driving the car.

"That's just the trouble with salesmen," she began. "And you know the part I hate the most? You can't insult them. They have no natural threshold of pride, like normal people. Jack looks typical—a Formica personality, clean and slick—you can keep him! He's one of the few I'll leave alone." She turned into the school parking lot, and the screech as we rounded the curb drowned out my sarcastic "Thanks!" Since the gym was only lit on one side, most of the parking lot was dark when we pulled in. "I'm gonna bust if I don't get to the loo," she said, and then she hit the big parked car so hard I gasped and popped the side seam of my new black leotard.

"Oh fuck! Well, hold on, now we'll have to walk a little bit farther." She backed off the bumper of the bluish car and smoothly pulled over to the far side of the parking lot and unwrapped her legs. "They should never make cars the same color as the nighttime—you really can't see them for shit! Come on, come on" . . . And later, when she saw the rip in my leotard, she hunted around among the ladies for a needle and then pulled a couple of the longest hairs out of her head so I could sew it up. "Human hair is invisible," she said. "It's cool —you can still get started on the exercises and nobody will be the wiser—human hair is stronger than anything—it'll hold you in—trust me." You could see the stitches glowing pinkly in the dark seam, however, and they hurt like tiny burrs all through the class. But when I washed the leotard the next day, the pink color rinsed out and then the stitches were indeed invisible.

Next, I remember her red hair floating against a big piece of carpet padding that one of the neighbors had put out for the large garbage pickup. Garbage picking had become her favorite shopping exercise when I tried to get her interested in cleaning her house, which didn't work all that well, but I felt I had to contribute something unique to this friendship, something to keep her away from Jack.

"Why would I want to *clean* it?" she asked, horrified, when I suggested a day of scrubbing. We only bought it for investment, and the trusty economy will put a special shine on it for me, you just wait. And besides, who has the time? Listen, I've got it—let's *collect* instead of clean. Then you can organize what we gather up—take your mind off dirt. Do you realize all the great stuff these stupid people around here are throwing out?" And so we would set out at dawn, crawling close to the curb in my unmarked station wagon before the poor people came over from across the river and picked the place clean. We were on our way back home, after getting a few toys and some wicker baskets, when she yelled, "Stop! Stop! I can really use that!" and she was out of the car before it had stopped moving. She threw herself on a giant pile of carpet padding and it closed around her like a soft fortune cookie, leaving only her legs still on the sidewalk. She scrambled out of it and the commotion caused it to grow some more, so that now it was as big as a small, pale whale. She stripped off her pea jacket to attack it again. She jumped astride it and sank up to her elbows.

"Don't just sit there—help me!" she yelled, her red head like a small bleeding wound in its side. I got out and embraced it with both my arms and tried to pick it up. It wouldn't move, couldn't be moved, and it was as heavy as the first time you ever tried to lift up your giant aunt, who was standing in front of the refrigerator pretending to guard it. It was overpoweringly moldy with urine and morning dew in each of its little pockmarks, but together we slowly stuffed it into the station wagon and drove it to her house. She put it on the back porch, where it sat breathing all last year like a doughy lump of unbaked bread. She said she wanted it to put under her blue shag rug to absorb the noise from her piano practice, because she was going to Juilliard in the fall if she could get in, and if she could stay in the neighborhood until then without cracking.

The next time she wanted to move was after the Avon Lady had organized a square-dance competition in their adjoining back yards, and Rosa, who was now the Avon Lady's cook, had dumped all the refried beans at the corner of the property, all over Maggie's wildflower preserve.

"It's not the mess; it's the dresses," she said when she pulled the duffel down to pack. "Nothing personal—I'll be gone out of here just as soon as I can get the place sold. I belong in the city—any city . . . See you around . . ." she said. But when the real-estate agent told her that, given today's inflation, her house was now worth ten thousand less than when she bought it, because of the condition she'd brought it to, she called me up for some ideas on how to clean it up. I knew eventually she'd need me for something—it was just a matter of time, and like the Gila monster, I could be very patient.

"Do you have any buckets, or brooms, or a vacuum cleaner down there?" I asked, dusting off the angel's left sleeve as we talked. The angel held my phone book open in her palms, and it was very convenient to lean back on her shoulder while I talked on the phone.

"Nah—just come down and talk to me—maybe you can convince me to go out and buy some. Or go buy me a wife somewhere. Besides, I've got a little surprise for you. Come right over, okay?"

I only had time to pack a small rubber football for Toby to play with, and when we got there, she had tacked a little sign to the front door: COME IN—IT'S OPEN. I'M IN THE BEDROOM. I pushed open the door, knocking over a bag of kitty litter, but left the sign up in case it wasn't meant for me.

"Come on up—I'm cleaning!" she called down when she heard two of the cats hissing at me. I found her in the bedroom, where she was sitting on the floor in such a big pile of clothes that she looked like one of Aunt Ruth's crocheted dolls for the bed, the ones with the impossibly big ruffled skirts. You could store a week's worth of dirty underwear under one of them, and then they'd start to smell just like a real person.

"Welcome to the Age of Acquirious," she said. "I was looking for something to wear to scrub in, and then I realized—Just how many Russian peasant blouses does any one person need? Why don't you look through some of this garbage for something you can use? Some of it's hardly ever been worn. God, what are you supposed to wear when you know you're going to be depressed? Here—see if this fits . . ." and she threw across to me a linen blouse embroidered all over in red cross-stitch, my first authentic piece of artistic clothing. Toby was bouncing his football and flopping into the piles happily, as if it were washday. Maggie burrowed deeper into the closet. "My mother sent it from the Ukraine. I'm afraid it's ponderously Polish, but it's nearly brand-new, and it was hideously expensive. Maybe you could do something with it—what do you think?"

I pulled it on over my turtleneck, and once I'd gotten my arms in and the sleeves buttoned, I turned and looked in Maggie's tilted pier glass. The blouse smelled as if Maggie were still in it, and if I squinted, I could really look a little like her: a shorter, squatter version, a funhouse Maggie.

"I don't know . . . you could cut off the sleeves, make it into a vest," she was saying. "You're pretty clever with sewing, right?" Before I could answer, Toby's brown rubber football bounced against my leg, and he looked up and around for it.

"Listen, I think Chuck's got the hots for you—"

And suddenly all was slow motion, there was dead silence, except for a persistent scratching sound, and before the edges of the room returned and the crowds began to cheer, I asked for an instant replay: Chuck's got the hots for you. For you. You.

I pictured myself picking up the little rubber football and running with it. All I would really need to do would be to make some plans for wholesome get-togethers with the four of us, and then there would be intimate moments pulled out of comfortable gatherings, and across a crowded room our eyes would lock, and I'd fall backward into his arms, our lips would touch with the excitement of crossed wires, but first . . . I had to throw Maggie off the track and keep her away from Jack, as well.

She was continuing: "He keeps asking when we're all going to get together, and I know it's not Jack he means. At least, I don't think so, although with Chuck you can never be sure of anything . . . anyway, wait until you see this! Don't say a word . . ." and then she was digging deep, deeper, into the closet. "Wait! I've got him here somewhere . . . where are you? Ah! Come out of there, you little bugger" . . . Toby popped up. "Christ, where did *you* come from?" she asked the back of his head. She turned back into the closet, leaned over with both hands extended, and then finally she caught it and held it up in front of her.

At first I thought it was a little white stuffed toy, the kind you put on your bed next to the lady in the big ruffled dress, but it was real, a squirming white Angora kitten whose eyes, while she held him, flashed with a red glow and then changed back to blue.

"He's for you. Here . . ." And I jumped back, horrified, as it reached a claw out for me.

"Nah!" And she pulled him back. Toby swiveled his head between us, and I threw him the football, suddenly embarrassed at the picture of a grown woman playing with such a silly little toy.

"Can I change my mind and keep him? We're already in love," she pleaded. "I can't resist him, I have to have him—and now Chuck says if one more animal comes into this house, he moves out. I tell you, I really considered that ultimatum for a while. I mean, this little cutie here can sleep in a pile of my socks and still be happy, right? Not stay out all night . . . never throw things at pauvre little me . . . I hate giving him up because Chuck says so! And damnit, I won't!" She paused again. "But I don't want to antagonize him any more than I have to right now . . ." She held the kitten at arm's length, out to me . . . "But I can give him lots and lots of love!" And she pulled it back, rocking him and kissing him between his squeezed-shut eyes. "Ha! Cat got your tongue? What do you think? Listen—you'd better go. You don't want to be around Chuck when he comes home and I tell him I've managed to spend ten thousand of our dollars without ever even leaving the house. So depressing!"

It was time to help her, I decided, so I pulled the peasant

blouse off, pushed up my sweater sleeves, and said, "Look at it this way—what you're calling depressing can be lucky, or even beautiful. Maybe you've hit rock bottom and there's nowhere to go now but up. That's from Salada."

"Salada who?"

"Tea—Salada tea."

"You read tea leaves? I didn't know that."

"Just the bags, not the leaves. Listen, let me help you with this mess."

She brightened. "You'll clean it up? All *right!* Now we're cooking! Maybe we could switch off on some projects together—the four of us—and Chuck and I will bring the good tea. What do you say? What can we name the cat? Let's think up something grand . . . I've got it! Archimedes! How's it go—give me a kitty long enough and I'll move the earth? Or is he the guy who did the original screw?" she asked, as I bent to clean up her mess.

A month later, Jack and I finished off our basement as a playroom for the kids; on the side we built a workshop for him and a sewing room for me. I have "before" and "after" pictures of the room in my scrapbook. The transformation is amazing, but no matter how cheery we tried to make it, I still knew it was the basement, and you can never trust a cellar. It's where the washtubs, the oil burner, and assorted other bad things are. It accumulates failure in wet boxes, and abandons all pretense to cracked, dirty windows and peeling paint. It is still the reminder of coming death to me, with its graveyard walls of dirt, vines growing into empty sockets, posts and beams getting eaten away by rot, by bugs, by age and weight, even if all that's behind the bleached luan paneling now. The real cellar is flaw, roots, potential neglected, the end of hope.

And I worried about our constructing a room down there because I thought it was symptomatic of other cosmetic improvements we were making since we had started seeing Chuck and Maggie. During the basement renovation, Chuck started coming over more and more to learn all about carpentry from Jack, he said, but, I think, after what Maggie said, that he also wanted to see me. I didn't believe any good ever came from asking friends to come into the cellar, however, because I could never trust anyone who wanted to sit in the cellar and, worse, pretend he was in a fancy room. Remember the room at the end of *2001*? That pathetic little shell of the imagination alone in the bleakest of black space, whirling away? A playroom in the basement is no different than that, if you ask me. It's like a fancy coffin in the ground.

Jack and Chuck seemed to have no such thoughts, of course, when they decided to change a corner of the playroom into an elaborate bar with swings hanging from the ceiling instead of bar stools.

"Now we can all be swingers," Jack joked over my head to Chuck once when they were taking a break to try out the new bar. I was on my hands and knees over in the TV section of the room, trying to scrub the black glue off the new floor tiles. I heard Jack whisse the caps off two Millers against his new custom-installed sunken bottle opener and I waited for the clatter of the caps falling into the coffee can he had installed to catch them. When one of them missed, he tried to adjust the can and slashed his arm so dangerously close to the wrist artery that he had to be rushed to the hospital for stitches. Before I could straighten up from the scrub bucket, Chuck had stopped the bleeding with one hand and slapped Jack in the face with the other to keep him from fainting. The only car around that day was Maggie's old Chevy, because ours was in the shop, so she drove him to the hospital, and all I could do to help was stay behind with the babies, because Maggie's brake boot was too small for me. I waited and cleaned up his blood before the kids messed in it, washed it out of the coffee can, where it was so deep the Miller cap was floating, and off the sunshine tile we had just installed. If it hadn't been for Chuck, who'd stopped the bleeding with his twisted shirt, Jack would probably have bled to death, a sacrifice to his own perfectionism in bottle-cap openers.

When he wasn't on the road selling, Jack was now jogging with Chuck on Wednesday nights. They had formed a sort of alliance in which Jack made himself forever in Chuck's debt for saving his life, something he said never happened to him during his whole tour in Vietnam. Chuck was the team doctor at the community college, and he had frightened Jack into worrying about a heart attack with stories of "men in their twenties who just keel over one day, and they were in great shape! What's going to happen to you?" Jack had changed in ways so subtle since he'd come back from Vietnam that I still had trouble understanding him sometimes, and this jogging was one typical example. He said he was afraid of getting old, of dying, of not knowing everyone in the neighborhood. When three stewardesses bought the old ocher house at the very end of the neighborhood, near the tennis courts, he and Chuck jogged down there, all the way past the train station, past the shutters the stewardesses always kept closed. Most of all, Jack mourned the fact that he hadn't been in college during the time of coed dorms and "free love"—he'd had to pay for it through the teeth, he said. Then suddenly he worked up a whole new jogging route that avoided the stewardesses' house when Maggie told him that they were lesbians. "God, you can't be sure of anything any more," he said, pulling on his third layer of sweatsocks. "Just yourself, you can only depend on yourself," and he kicked the beard of snow off the front doorstop and jogged off into the night. He worried more and more about missing something now, so he puffed around and around the neighborhood with Chuck, waved goodbye to him under the cheery coach lantern at our front door, and then collapsed, heaving, into the breakfast booth, for the hot chocolate I had kept warmed at the perfect temperature for him. He wanted it all now, health as well as whipped cream.

I thought Aunt Ruth was finally fading into the background, since so much of the foreground was being taken up with the Mathesons. If Maggie cleaned the house more after knowing me, I didn't particularly notice the difference, but I did notice that I wasn't as satisfied as much any more with simply cleaning my house, and then cleaning it again, just for Aunt Ruth. The ironing, the ironing, was fast becoming the irony, the irony. I felt that I was giving all my life to the maintenance of my carpets, my kids, and the kitchen sink. The fragile tapestries of thought I would weave as I moved slowly through the living room with throbbing vacuum tube in hand, protected by my miraculous circle of noise, would then seem to disappear when the machine stopped, sucked away by something even stronger than the vacuum. And it wasn't as much fun any more, now that Aunt Ruth would never again creep up on me when I was supposed to be cleaning. I used to sing under the bed in the dust, with the big Hoover blowing away like a wind machine beside me. Once, she crept in, picked up the tube from the floor, and with a savage thrust poked me out from under the bed, beat me out the back door, and locked it; and it was freezing cold out there. I'm still afraid of being stuck outside without a sweater, and I still don't know what made her madder—the fact that I was lazy or the fact that I was happy. Now I was trying to be a little lazy, if that would make me happy, because in spite of our new friendship with Maggie and Chuck, I was feeling sadder and more empty than the day that Glynnis told me to just leave the Corning Ware casserole in her mailbox when I was finished with it. Don't call us, we'll call you; and they never call back.

We played bridge with Chuck and Maggie, saw X-rated movies with them, and played doubles on the deserted tennis courts behind our neighborhood in the dead of winter. It was so cold last February that when I leaned over to pick up the ball I had missed, big wet drops of warm salty stuff would fall out of my nose onto the ground. I remember looking up from trying to find my ball by breaking the frozen weeds with my racquet. Maggie was suddenly standing very close to me, smiling, and holding a new metal racquet with a red bow tied on it. It absorbed the only gleam of light that sunless day. She was so skinny that she could wear two pairs of pants to keep warm without strangling at the waist.

"Happy Birthday," she said.

"Where did this come from?" I asked.

"From Jack."

Jack smiled when I thanked him and said, "It was nothing," but I thought then that something was up between the two of them. He bought a new sports car in the spring, and she bought an antique one a few weeks later. Hers was an old MG the color and shine of a candy apple.

The first time she ever drove it was also the first time we ever had a formal dinner party. They were nearly an hour late, because the car wouldn't start and Maggie wouldn't leave it in the driveway and walk over. While we waited for them, we had second, and then third, drinks with the gardening neighbor and her husband on our side porch, beside the patio. As we sipped our drinks and watched the street, it was the softness of the early evening that was by far the most interesting presence in our small group. It was that moment in the season when spring seems exposed, uncovered, nearly obscene in its earliness; not ready yet, yet too delicious to wait for any longer. To sit on the porch in early April like that gave me the same kind of feeling I get when I eat the pudding I'm cooking before it bubbles, or peel a Polaroid picture from its backing before it's ready. Or maybe it was just because Chuck was coming over and we'd get him drinking, and then, there would be no telling what could happen.

I'd been introduced to the gardening neighbor's husband twice by that time, and I still couldn't remember his first name. My biggest fear, as I finished my third gin-and-tonic, was that I'd ask him a second time what he did at the IRS, and then forget what he said about that again, too. I can't take a man who wears a slippery white short-sleeved shirt seriously, especially if he wears an undershirt and has a hard leather case for his sunglass snap-ons in his breast pocket. When we finished that round of drinks, Jack suggested a quick tour of our property before the realization that we'd been stood up by Maggie and Chuck took over completely and soured the creamed spinach even before we sat down to eat. Jack is an excellent host, and the only rule he follows is to make the drinks so strong that you wince. It works, too. Those who need the alcohol are grateful, those who are too shy get drunk, and those who don't like it complain. "If I'm too potent for you, I'll water it down," he always says as he hands out drinks, and someday I'm going to have a T-shirt printed with that saying on it for him.

By the time Maggie puttered past our patio with a merry honk of her new antique horn, I'd almost begun to wish she'd stayed home, because the gardening neighbor was admiring my strawflower arrangement in the living room and I hated to give up the spotlight. But everyone rushed to the driveway, gathered around the new car, stroked it, and while Maggie modeled it, I slipped into the kitchen to check on the roast. I heard sputters of laughter from the driveway as I basted the lamb and turned on the vegetables, and by the time I was putting the salad out, Jack had already gotten drinks out to the Mathesons.

By now the dinner was out of my control. The salad course was floating away because Archimedes had been packed into the car, too, so that the motor could be said to purr like a kitten, and now he was under the table, snagging his claws in the ends of my lace tablecloth. Chuck picked him up and put him on the porch during soup, but there he scratched the screen and nearly chilled the meat with the sound, so during dessert, Jack put him into the basement playroom.

"Don't *worry* so much!" He patted my sweaty shoulder as he walked past my chair.

"It takes practice not to worry about details," Maggie said, sipping her wine. "I've become expert."

I saw the glance pass between the gardening neighbor and her husband, as she handed over the sugar to him and he spooned out a precise teaspoon into his cup. The two neighbors sat like twin library lions, quiet and substantial, while Maggie spoke in quick, graffiti-like strokes.

"I think being sloppy just takes practice, like anything else, Maybe if you and Jack traveled, you wouldn't care so much about the fate of a single lace tablecloth."

"That won't help," I ventured. "A while back, when Jack and I went to the Marriage Encounter—"

"You went to one of those things?" Chuck asked.

"Did it work?" someone else asked, putting down a cup.

Suddenly the floor was mine. I'd said something of undeniable interest. Or else, they were all being nice to me because I'd just fed them.

"What's it do—I can't keep these things straight—does it make you Total or Perfect?" Maggie asked the whole table.

"You're missing the point," I said.

"It's just a weekend retreat," Jack said.

"A weak-end retread," Maggie said to him.

"Let her tell what happened—*I'm* interested," said the gardening neighbor.

They turned to me again, and I took a breath. "My big treat to myself was going to be to make it seem like a vacation from all my jobs. I wasn't going to do any folding or scouring or straightening up, and I figured some new thoughts would rush in to fill the vacuum," I said, folding and refolding my flowered napkin.

"That's logical," he said. One of the men.

"Well, as we were going up to our room, I noticed a piece of white string curled into the raised nylon pattern in the blue carpet outside our door, and I thought to myself, I'm not going to pick up that string. I'm not going to clean anybody's house for the whole weekend, and I'll start with that string—by leaving it alone."

"Good thinking," Maggie said, finishing her wine. She looked to Jack for more, and he smiled at her fingers on the glass as he filled it, right up to the brim.

"Besides, somebody else would do it if I didn't—why should I always be the one to pick up after everyone? Makes sense, right?" No one answered, so I continued, making it into a story: "Well, obviously no one else saw the string, and it sat there for the whole next day. During naptime I became obsessed with it—the way it curled into the carpet, and at the same time protected itself from being swept away on someone's shoe. It was nestled there like a worm, winding into my thoughts, ruining my concentration on interpersonal dialoguing—"

"What in the hell is that?"

"Talking. And messing up my ability to contribute much to the mutual assessment of tacit commitment—"

"Wha . . . ?"

"*Not* talking."

"Listen, this is important," Chuck said, looking pointedly at Maggie, who was twirling her fork into the lace.

"But why do they call everything by those idiot titles?" Maggie asked.

"Because it costs money," Jack answered. "Continue, continue—this is all news to me."

"By nighttime, I saw it snaking through my dreams, back and forth, in and out—it was in the marbleized binding of the Bible in the room, and on the pattern of my suitcase lid. It's a plastic bubbly lid, blue, just like the rug, with a white scratch in it that's curved in the same exact wavy pattern of the string in the carpet. By that time we were doing non-verbal communication, I was finger-painting the string, making it out of clay, and curving it into a winding shape, and of course, you thought I was trying to say penis, but that I was too repressed."

"Weren't you?" Jack asked, actually surprised.

"Well, it all sounds pretty neurotic to me. What do you think, Chuck, do we pack her off in the wagon?" Maggie asked.

"This is a medically valid infirmity—I've read case histories of people who get totally obsessed, possessed even, with a single detail . . ."

"So—are you? Repressed? I mean, more than's obvious?" she repeated.

"Do you ever get migraine headaches?" Chuck asked, obviously concerned.

"Is there an ending to this cliff-hanger of a tale? Did anyone ever pick the damn thing up?" asked the gardening neighbor's husband.

"I'm coming to it—wait. All through the mass of renewal at the end of the encounter, I was mesmerized by the priest's twisted and knotted white rope belt on his vestment, and I'm sure that's where the string had come from in the first place . . ."

"Wouldn't you just love to seduce a priest?" Maggie asked.

"I'm sure he was littering the whole retreat house with his strings. When we were packing to go, I had an urge to bare my soul and tell Jack about the problem."

"You sure as hell should have. Let him know what he's got on his hands," Chuck said, unwrapping a long, thick, hefty cigar.

"Poor Jack," said Maggie.

"So why didn't you tell me? That's really stupid!"

"But you were reading your journal of commitment so peacefully in the window seat while you waited for me to pack us up that I couldn't disturb you. You looked so comforted—"

"Damn right I was comforted—we paid over three hundred dollars."

"And no matter what, comfort like that is fleeting."

"So? What happened?" asked the gardening neighbor.

"That night back home in bed, I couldn't consider having sex, because by now I was panicked—why had the string been in front of *my* door? Was it a personal test? And if so, had I failed by not picking it up? And the worst part, I realize now, is if I had gone ahead and picked the string right up, as is my normal habit, I'd never have given it a second thought. So that's why I clean."

"O . . . *kay*. So!" Maggie looked up, and around, as if she'd just broken through the water into fresh air. She looked to Jack.

"Would anyone like an after-dinner drink?" Jack asked, standing up and gathering a few butter plates. And then the spotlight snapped out, and the second cup of coffee was passed around, and I'd gone too far, I could feel it. I couldn't get back into the group fast enough, and so the currents at the table parted, quite naturally, the way your hair will when the hair spray wears off. Chuck was talking to the other husband, and Maggie and Jack were comparing sports cars.

The gardening neighbor turned to me and said, "I like your ideas about cleaning—you say them very well. You must read a lot."

"Oh, I do, I do. I also watch TV, and I saw an episode of *Kung Fu* that said to consider cleaning as a humbling act that allows your spirit to rise the more you are disciplined to the world around you."

"Sickening!" Maggie broke in, turning her chair toward us. "That's insane! Admit it—it's a never-ending job, and what kind of satisfaction can you get from a job you can't get done?"

"That's just it—the Orientals rake sand into patterns in their garden. I scour the sink every day. Then Jack dumps his coffee grounds in, and Debbie throws in the jelly knife, and the wind has blown the gardener's patterns away. I have a job—there is something so comforting about the person who picks things up and arranges, don't you think? It's the opposite of being an iconoclast—I think of myself as an iconokeeper."

"Maybe Tupperware will come out with a whole line of you."

"I think that's a beautiful thought," the gardening neighbor said, and Maggie stared at her, making her eyes cross a little. It wouldn't have been noticeable unless you knew Maggie's typical expression of contempt.

"I guess that's proof, then, if two of you agree," she said. "You both are certifiable. It's so depressing! Maybe I could steal Rosa for a week or two. Help her keep beans on the table."

"If Rosa comes and cleans up your messes, she'll be stronger than you, because she'll be doing something you admit you can't do," I said. "Besides, she'll know everything about you in the world, after having gone through all your stuff—do you want somebody that close? Even a cat covers up its trail—"

"Shit! The cat! I forgot all about him down there—what do you think he's messed into this time? Which reminds me—I have to brush him every single day so he doesn't develop a fur ball and die! Can you believe it! Every day! I knew I should have given him to you—it'd give you something new and exciting to clean."

"See! That's exactly what I mean! Cleaning is a matter of life and death: all life means is not being dirt. The minute a thing dies, it gets stinky, smelly, dirty, rotten—it becomes a piece of garbage, and it has to be cleaned up."

"You're really a mental, you know? I have better things to do with my time than think about garbage. My parents paid a fortune for my education—and you're telling me to wash floors. You know, you sound like one of those people I've always heard about but never believed I'd ever meet. Someone comes bleeding their guts out into your kitchen and you try to mop it up before you even go to help the wounded."

And then, in front of everybody, but seen by no one but me, Chuck winked at me.

The next day, I went down to visit Chuck while Maggie was at her music lesson. My excuse was that I was taking Toby for a walk. He was walking, loosely speaking, beside me, and stirring up leaves that were partially decomposed, and we got to the end of the street by a series of diminishing arcs, because I was never really sure if I should be visiting Chuck at all. I was pretending to follow Toby, who hadn't yet learned how to go in reverse—I just pointed him in the direction of Maggie's, said "Cornflakes," and he walked.

I saw Chuck's head moving back and forth, back and forth, in the underbrush at the back of his property before I got to the swinging gate in the split-rail fence he had put up to mark off his front yard from the Avon Man's. As I got nearer, I could see he was carrying bundles and placing them at the base of a smoldering pile of twigs that was more smoke than blaze. I lifted Toby over the gate and then stepped over the lowest part myself, because the gate had never worked properly.

We silently entered Matheson territory and almost got to the house before Chuck heard us and turned and stared. Twigs fell from the bundle he was holding, and as we got closer, Archimedes saw the movement and broke away from his leash on the post. He clawed on the legs of Chuck's brown corduroy pants and nearly knocked him over with the force of his lunge. Chuck kicked him away, and then I finally realized what it was about Chuck that was driving me crazy. It was the pants—his brown pants. There was a boy in the seventh grade who wore the same exact pair of pants, brown corduroys, to school. Each day, every day, for the entire year. The first few days no one noticed, of course, and treated him just like anyone else. Then, after a week, then two weeks, kids who had rashly made friends with him thinking he was normal were the first to point out the pants to others, so that they wouldn't be lumped in with him any more by mistake. By Christmas he was an outcast, and the seat of his pants had become shiny like a burned muffin bottom. It was rumored that his parents had enough money, and Jo Anne Smolla, the nicest girl in class, suggested there might be several pairs of brown corduroys and that he changed his pants as often as anyone else, but unnoticed.

Like belling the cat, the job of chalking his belt loop in back so that there would be no mistake about the pants fell to Michael McBurney. He was the most timid boy in the class, a kid whose glasses broke when they fell off into the water fountain during recess, and who still occasionally sat at lunch with the brown corduroys because he had nothing particularly to lose. Then, by Valentine's Day, the chalk mark was nearly rubbed off, but still clearly visible on the brown corduroy belt loop, especially when he bent over his galoshes in the cloakroom, and Michael McBurney was promoted to flipping baseball cards with the Big Three. When spring came, the pants were patched at the knee and nobody really cared any more; Michael was demoted by natural inferiority nearly back to his old status, and William Wharton, who wore the brown corduroys, skipped the eighth grade and went to Georgetown University after high school, and now he's a brain surgeon in Chicago.

"Maggie's not home," he was saying, while picking up the twigs. Then he was on his knees, blowing on the fire, trying to get it restarted.

"I know. I was trying to get Toby around the block in less than an afternoon, and he seems to think cornflakes fall out of the heavens here . . ."

"Humph! Well! Is Jack home? I could use some help back here. I'm getting rid of this jungle so Riva won't break her neck out here in the summer." It's funny how people are supposed to be certain places, and unless they stay there, where they're supposed to be, things don't go right. For instance, Chuck was supposed to be at work, and I was supposed to visit only Maggie at this address. So maybe I was mistaken about everything—about Chuck wanting to see me when he came over to work with Jack. Or maybe Maggie was mistaken about Chuck liking me. Or maybe I was mistaken about Maggie, or Jack. So I took Toby, who was still asking for cornflakes, home. I wasn't sure just what was wrong, but something was.

Because Jack was away so much, Maggie eventually knew more about my life than he did, and whenever you have to rewrite history for a new person, it's hard not to believe the new version yourself. So it was quite easy for us to plan a surprise party for my new version of Jack in June and to start fantasizing at the same time about how much fun an orgy would be, given the kinds of husbands we had in these new versions. And there was no way the new or the old Jack could ever know about it.

In fact, I think our orgy plans were the most creative things Maggie and I ever did together. We spent long hours on the phone, which I had snaked around the kitchen corner past the angel so I could talk darkly down on the cellar steps and not be heard. Our talks progressed from the kind of conversation in which we each just waited our turn to talk, to say a set piece that had been thought through many times before, following the same procedure that you used to follow for jump rope: you waited your turn to jump in, recite a rhyme, and then jump out. Then we started telling each other some less rehearsed thoughts, until finally we had arrived at ideas that were mutually created on the spot, so dependent were they on our collaboration for their existence. The orgy was born this way.

But the surprise party was more Maggie's idea than mine, and for reasons I couldn't figure out at the time, Jack wasn't surprised at all. I think the month in which a person is born does something to his personality, and that birthday party convinced me that this theory is correct. Jack had no way of knowing about it, yet even after I had hidden people behind the couches and in the coat closet, he never even tried to act surprised. I consider this blasé attitude a result of his being born when the world is lush. The months of April and May have just dumped all their riches into his birthday in June and there's simply more and more to follow—he knows that. June expects it, and it continues, for the rest of the summer. Which explains why Jack takes everything for granted, why he always believes his ship will come in, that there's another train if he misses this one, and now he even drives a company car. While I, born in February, am forever frostbitten, yet hopeful, because I'm near enough to spring to believe in it but too far away from it to feel its warmth. And Maggie! Maggie makes me so sick! She was born into the end of August, so for her, everything is ripe, just waiting for the picking, and the harvest is coming. She goes through life gathering, gathering, with her cheeks full.

Now, the party seemed to have been a success, in spite of Jack's lack of surprise. I was spending a greater part of it in the kitchen, trying to get drunk, because I was feeling as if all my work had come to nothing. The real reason I had wanted to give this party at all was so Jack would appreciate me and feel obligated in some way—I wanted him to need me for something. I was finishing my second gin-and-tonic when Chuck came into the kitchen.

"Drinking alone is a mortal sin, you know," he said, much too cheerfully for me. "And you shouldn't be drinking this stuff—it'll rot your insides." Chuck, like Maggie, was pretty much what you'd expect—there is a health fad, and they join up. Maggie always says that Chuck is plain-looking compared to Jack, and she is probably right, but I found him scruffy and comfortable, like one of those booths in a college soda shop where everyone has carved his initials. And anyway, ever since Maggie called him a Formica personality, Jack's smelled funny to me.

"Here, let me make you something you'll like," Chuck said, and with a flourish, he was kneeling in front of the open refrigerator and digging around in the vegetable bin for bananas, which I hate. Chuck's always kneeling around me—

maybe this is a sign. When he stood up, he was sweating across his delicate upper lip, so he took off his shirt and draped it over a chair. "Being healthy is good hard work." He smiled, and turned to the blender, stuffing in the banana. In spite of everything I'd tried to stop thinking about him, his naked back still made me want to grab at him. It was so warm, so supple, with its broad shoulders and the muscles near his arms moving in rhythm. His curls curved down from the nape of his neck like a manicured garden path and up from his belt like a black puff of smoke. I got my drink back from the drainboard and downed it before he even turned around.

"Here, try some of this," he said, and poured a yellowish slush from the blender into a plastic highball glass.

"What's in it?" I asked, because he expected me to, and stuck my finger in the foam and licked it off, because he expected me to do that, too. The most exciting part is walking out to the dance floor and waiting while the music plays, knowing you can start if you want to. We tease each other as a kind gesture, sensing that our mates are not tearing down any doors to keep us apart.

"Don't worry about what's in it—just drink it. It's good for you—it'll put hair on your chest." I looked at his chest, naturally, which was smooth and tanned, just two round nipples breaking up the wide expanse of skin.

"So what's it done for you lately?"

He smiled, his teeth as white as they were straight. "Let me show you sometime."

I sensed a new level of the tease. Was something up? And so, just for insurance, I dumped a big plop of gin into the drink and the first sip stung as if it were medicine. Maggie came in to check on the ice and asked me to take the cake out of the freezer in ten minutes, all without looking at Chuck. He began chopping the limes while she was talking to me, smashing the knife into them with a great vigor, until they were just a green pulp when she left. Poor Chuck! There is something so pathetic and inviting about a man who is married, worse, second-married, and worse still, Open Married. He seems like a bull with three little picador swords bleeding from his neck.

Finally, the gin was beginning to work and the room was starting its comfortable blur around the edge. Chuck was lining up the plastic glasses on the counter, and he bumped into me when he leaned over the trash can, and then when he closed the refrigerator he softly brushed my arm. I felt the hairs stand up like fur stroked the wrong way and the gargoyle smile in my palm throbbed gently. I sipped again, for the courage to push him past teasing me. Jack came in with an empty glass and two bottles of wine under his arm. He kissed me on the forehead, which he never does when we're alone.

"So we meet again," he said to me, or to the stove against which I was leaning. "Why don't you come out and talk to Maggie—she's all upset about something." I watched him put the bottles in the refrigerator, carefully laying them down with their labels up, so that they were beside some of the salad that I keep for Maggie when she comes over hungry. He brushed a speck off the nearest bottle—Jack's the neat-freak, not me, by the way.

"So you're enjoying your party?" I asked him.

"Maggie and you have really knocked yourselves out."

"Maggie and me? *Maggie* and me? Don't you have your order a little screwed up?" When he blushed, which he hardly ever does, I knew I'd hit pay dirt, even if I didn't want to. There was definitely something up. Chuck was breathing so hard that we both could hear him, and when I looked over at him, he was doing deep knee bends against the counter. Jack looked at him and he straightened up, his face red.

"Let me freshen your drink," Chuck said, reaching across Jack, and when he took my glass he didn't touch his fingers to mine.

Jack was getting angry, so he smiled. "Why don't you bring your drink out to the living room—it looks as if you're hiding in here, you two." He was pouring some Dubonnet into a curved glass, a real glass, and then he sliced a half moon of lemon peel and carefully twisted it over the wine, letting the oil spray all over the golden surface, and then he dropped the spiral into the liquid.

"Whose drink?"

"Maggie's of course," I said to no one in particular, and then sipped twice at my drink and waited until Jack left the room before starting the timer for the cake. The gin was starting to slow me down, to make me more aware of the movement around me, to give me the power to speak over the ticking. It even started to taste better. It made me less worried, more objective, at least in the beginning. The second drink is always easier than the first, and the third is positively a pleasure. I dumped my used ice cubes and limes into the garbage and opened the cabinet for a real glass, too. I never cry. The last time I ever did was when I swallowed an ice cube whole and Aunt Ruth scalded her hands in the hottest water from the faucet and laid them against my throat to stroke the diamond edges into melting faster. "Crying's only going to make it hurt more," she said, frantic. I want the same things that Maggie has. I made myself a new drink very carefully and concentrated on Chuck's hands and tried to see if I could get him to touch me again, this time not by accident on his part but by design on my part. Just by thinking, directing him. I put my drink down on the counter and rested one hand beside it. He was washing the plastic glasses, looking for cracks, holding one up to the light, rubbing for spots. I took another sip. He had to feel my eyes on his bare shoulders, down one muscled arm, commanding it to move, come to me, closer, closer. My hand was warm, waiting. He set the glass down on the counter, the cloth near my hand. My wedding ring glinted in the light, and his hand seemed to be pulled nearer and nearer, as if our rings were magnetized. His eyes were on the floor, and then they slid up my leg, and I could feel bubbles skimming up my silky body, I could feel his blue eyes dragging up until they met mine and he held me to them, to the blue in them, to the moist blue where I could swim, deep in his blue eyes, and I could hear my own breathing . . . the clock . . . and then the timer went off like an angry wasp and Chuck jumped back as if he had been stung. His face was as red as mine and those ten minutes had just whooshed by us, quick as a hypnotic trance, unconnected to the tyranny of the clock.

*Salada says that happiness is a way sta-*tion between too little and too much, and this thought can bring us to the fateful night of the orgy. But still we need details before we get right into it. Maggie always laughs when I say the truth is in the details, but I got that one from Salada, too, and they haven't been wrong yet. So, some details.

How did we set it up? Simple. Jack was away, of course, and Chuck didn't care—he wanted to believe Maggie when she told him she was going to spend the night at my house because she had to get away from the kids for a while, and he even baby-sat all four kids for us. See how simple? And then Maggie knew a few people from Juilliard and they didn't care about the missing husbands—a party is a party, and we promised to feed them. And that's how the Michelob got into my refrigerator. It wasn't any big deal, really, just a few guys she studied with, one girl who played bass and one who wrote music, and the heat of that Indian-summer evening, which really helped us to pretend that we were some place else.

We drove over to the A & P as soon as we left the kids with Chuck. The sun was setting right into the windshield, a tear-jerking blaze of white light—the kind of flaming light that must have given Adam and Eve pause when they turned for one last look at the fire-barred gates of Eden. We were still euphemistically calling it a party, not an orgy, and although we really needed only wine and beer and a few things to eat that would make you thirsty, we had planned to stay at the market until the sun burned down past the giant picture windows at the checkout counter and quietly sank before we came home, so we could unload the groceries in the dark.

At the liquor store, the clerk stared at Maggie shining in a puddle of Chablis light in the glass doorway, bit off a fingernail, and insisted I buy the wine because she wasn't, *couldn't* be old enough. While they talked about whether 1968 was a good year for *anything*, I went over to the market, got a shopping cart, came back, and loaded it up with the wine. I was packing the bottles carefully in the back of the station wagon when Maggie backed through the glass doors of the liquor store waving with her free arm.

"Here's another bottle—compliments. He's gonna stop by later—we can always use an extra wanga-wanga, right? Let's see—we still have an hour and a half to kill—let's hit the market for a while."

"Are you going to invite all the ladies at the checkout when we go in?" I asked, slamming the tailgate.

"Hey, calm down. Calm down! Don't be so nervous—things are gonna go fine . . ."

"He could be an ax murderer, for all you know." I opened a bottle of malt liquor and drank it down, right there in the golden parking lot. "Or he could know Jack, for all you know . . ."

"No problem, really! I used to go out with him. I knew I knew him from somewhere—we went to junior high school together. He's still trying to get it together as an actor, so he'll fit right in, if you'll pardon the expression."

I burped a warm bubble of beer. I love to burp. "Let's do the market and get this show on the road," I said, following her through the automatic rubber-hinged doors, over to the fruit.

"I hate fruit debris," she said, and while I was picking among the tangerines, she wheeled smoothly past the cornucopia counters, spinning wire wheels around the corner, and I heard a crash, the tinkle of silvery laughter, and then the voice of Sherry, the prettiest neighbor. I wheeled over behind the pickles and relishes to listen.

"Why, hello, Mary Margaret!" I heard Sherry say. "And what brings you to our humble market? I thought you only shopped the health-food stores."

"I'm slumming, forgive me," Maggie said.

"And how's your mom? Is she still as beautiful as ever?" Sherry asked.

"Last I looked, she was doing fine— Excuse me, Sherry, but I'm in a bit of a hurry . . . see you around?"

"Oh, I'm sorry—but wait a sec, Mary Margaret . . . We miss you at the club—why don't you stop by again one of these days. Frankly, nobody can cheat the way you do and never get caught. We've lost the championship now for three years running—have you heard?"

"Well, it all depends on what I'm doing this fall with my music. Listen, I'll see you around, okay?"

When I caught up to Maggie, she was filling her cart with nuts. "Which do you like better: pistachios or cashews? What the hell, it's an orgy," she said, and threw both in. Then some peanuts.

"Shhhhh—*Mary Margaret!* I didn't know you knew Sherry—I've only heard of her, I've never met her. And please don't shout the word 'orgy.' "

"Are you kidding? Our mothers made their debuts together—I've always lived here, except in the last few years. We moved away when Daddy got promoted and Mother didn't. But my little intrigue with Sherry goes back years—we went to the same schools, all the way through. How about popcorn? You can't lose with all that hot air, right?"

And then, suddenly we were at the oils. "Crisco, Mazola—for the classy party of oil repute. Should we? Well, why not," she said, and reached for a tall bottle of safflower oil. "We might as well be healthy about it, although if we're really going to get down to it, honey is a hell of a lot tastier."

Then she leaned over my shopping cart. "What have you got here so far? Ha! Well . . . well. Have *you* ever got a feelthy mind! This is incredible! Butter—of course. Grapes—cute. And look at this, will you—this is absolutely gynecological!" And she held up the Reddi Wip with the dispenser tip that they say is for shooting into the bottom parts of parfaits. The cheeses that I had picked out had no significance other than I liked the laughing cow face and I thought maybe I could do something with the little cardboard container afterward. I'd also bought two dozen candles, so my stretch marks would be less obvious in the darker atmosphere, and by the time the stuff was rolling on the conveyor belt past the watchful eyes of the computer read-out and a dark-haired clerk named Lolly, I was sure we'd be arrested for lewdness. After checking out most of the items without raising her head, the woman suddenly rang the bell on her cash register and held up the Reddi Wip, and I was sure that one went too far—I thought we were done for. But instead of Joyce Brothers, another clerk came running over, took the can for a price check, and then yelled out $1.35 from somewhere within the store. Then we were finished, and I quickly bagged our guilty groceries while Maggie paid, and we walked out with our equipment in two brown paper wrappers.

I put the candles everywhere and we set up the Passout game with cheese and beer on Aunt Ruth's crazy quilt, which I had spread over the living-room carpet. I thought to kill two ghostly birds of guilt with one stone that way, and I was also afraid that any stains would be hard to get out of the gold rug, whereas they could never be seen at all in the dark colors of the quilt. And I was going to create my own crazy quilt, a live one out of real people, because she hadn't cornered the market on crazy—there was still time for me.

Guilty? Of course, I felt guilty. There can be no sin without guilt. I knew I wanted to sin, to make myself feel so bad that I would then have something to fix up, rather than just let things get worse and worse and let Jack and Maggie and Chuck keep drifting in and out of my life whenever they wanted to. At least Jack might think about me a little more when he was on the road, once he found out about this, if he found out about this.

I had also learned how to drink away most of the debilitating guilt that can stop you before you start, and I could do it in a half hour or so, give or take a few minutes. And I suspected Maggie, who wouldn't say if I asked, of fooling around with Jack, who would certainly never say. I didn't want to risk sounding paranoid or, worse, give anybody the idea if they hadn't thought of it before, but I can remember from high school that you can never trust a girlfriend if she happens to want your boyfriend. She'll feel bad, maybe, but she'll go ahead and take him anyway—it's biology. And a part of me thought that Maggie might stay a little longer in the neighborhood if the orgy was interesting enough, and I was sick of teasing Chuck, or had it turned around and now he was teasing me? And the tension of preserving my saintly marriage virginity was getting to me, especially since I thought that this marriage was the reason I was frigid in the first place.

Reasons enough? Or you could just say I went and did it, without so much as a glance at the street mail, which was coming at me with Special Delivery intensity. When you're suddenly going faster than you ever have before, you need every sign you can get, and you ignore them at your own risk. I noticed for the first time that afternoon that the Salada messages were shaped like little red stop signs. I ignored them. On my way home from the market, I noticed that every single light was red when I got to it, and I almost hit a squirrel. But sometimes you have to do something just to be bad, so you have new material to work with.

As it got nearer to eight o'clock, my resolve was softening as fast as the cheeses I was trying to unwrap and arrange on lettuce leaves.

"Let us begin. Brethren, we are gathered here together to join this man and this woman . . ."

"Why don't we just cancel the whole thing and go and see a dirty movie, instead—then there won't be any mess to clean up," I said to Maggie, who was winding herself into a peach-colored sari in front of the quiet little fire I had carefully laid that afternoon.

"We can't," she said, around the pins in her mouth. "I don't have any of their numbers—they live off campus and in lofts, on the edges of things, probably, and I'm sure they've already left, anyway. It's nearly an hour's drive from the city . . .

Here—can you help me with this?"

"This is really stupid!" I said, wiping the cheese off on the back of the sari.

"I thought it was right clever. You know: peachy-keen, loose, love means never having to say you're sari; sari, Charlie . . ."

"The phone numbers—not getting the phone numbers! What if Jack called and said he would be home early? How could we keep them from coming, then?"

"Well, remember, they're all musicians, first of all, and nothing can stop musicians from coming, heh, heh . . . and secondly, we'd simply sit around and pretend to play chamber music until old Jack Frost fell asleep on us, and then we could still get down to the business at hand."

"Jack Frost? Why Jack Frost? He's more like Jack-be-nimble, Jack-be-quick, if you ask me. Which reminds me—what else can I stick candles in so they won't drip all over the furniture?"

"Are you serious? He's enough to make anybody frigid, believe me. Just stick them in little glasses. Do you have any brandy snifters? *No*? Really? Egg cups? How about if you put them into fruit halves—just slice an apple or an orange in half and put it in a saucer, then dig out a space in the top for the candle, and it's soggy enough so there won't be a fire if it gets knocked over in the heat of passion; then you've got a disposable in spite of yourself. You can throw the whole thing out with tomorrow's mail. But *you* do it—I can't stand pieces of fruit lying around. I'll tell you one thing, though. Should this thing be pinned under my armpit or under my breast? Who cares? Right? Are you there?"

"I hate to dig out the pulp of stuff—it's such a waste. Go on, go on . . ."

"I'll tell you one thing, he sure ain't Jack the Pumpkin Eater, is he?"

I couldn't believe we were having this conversation, or even if we were both talking about the same thing. I looked very carefully for my next question, as if we were playing pick-up sticks. "Are you speaking from personal experience—about Jack, I mean?" I began, carefully clattering the extra ashtrays when she collapsed to her knees on the quilt in front of the fire.

"Shhhh—let's be quiet now and cleanse our minds—we're getting too silly. Let's let this experience come and enter unobstructed . . ."

But unfortunately, the toilet was still obstructed with Toby's last diaper before I hurried him down to Maggie's, so I was in the bathroom with my hands and mind in the toilet when the party actually began. I heard Maggie laugh with the first group that blew in when she opened the door. "Pizza!" she said. "That's really clever—do we eat it, or do we all get down and wallow in it?"

My partner in the Passout game was a shy pianist from Michigan who seemed amazed at my breasts, which he could get a glimpse of each time I reached for the dice. I had wanted to be more subtle, but since I've had very little practice at dressing like a loose woman, the halter I made didn't fit properly and my whole breast, rather than just the cleavage, showed. So I found myself being whisked along by the racing subliminal messages I was sending out like a person behind a runaway St. Bernard. When the card said *Drink*, he gulped down several swallows from the Mateus bottle, and when the card said *Kiss*, he grabbed me by the arm and cut his tongue through my lips so that I swallowed more of his wine. The object of Passout is to see who can drink the most liquor the fastest and still stand up. The winner gets to clean up the messes made by the losers.

The first person to get sick was the girl who wrote music, probably because she was the most sensitive. Her partner, a tall blond, who was either also sick or just anemic, leaned sympathetically against the bathroom door waiting for her, helped her into her jacket, and then quietly closed the back door behind them both after steering her through it. They were dull, anyway. The bass player was the first person to take off her clothes, because she wanted her partner to stand behind her and pretend she was a bass fiddle herself and play on her while he sang. Her partner was the clerk from the liquor store, and because he had no musical talent, it was painful to watch him pretend.

So, the next time I went into the kitchen for more beer, I pulled Amanda's kaleidoscope out from behind the tea canister and brought it into the living room just as the bass player was leaving. The clerk was now trying to play with Maggie's toes, but she kept pushing him away with her knee while she and her partner tangled in the sari. I aimed the kaleidoscope at the four people left on the floor and spun them up into a compote of peach, silk, fuzz, and pepperoni, with candles spinning like flaming batons on the Fourth of July in Anytown. When I heard bells ringing, I saw the peach pieces crawl out of the mosaic, and while someone was unbuttoning my jeans, I heard Maggie say, "I'll get that." Then I heard her yell, "Nothing's going on, Chucky baby! You've got a small, dirty little mind—you think I'm going to become a homo just so I can wait around for you—well, forget it, sucker!" She hung the phone up with a sharp twist of her wrist, and the pages in the angel's hand fluttered.

Then I was kissing someone again and I was only able to watch Maggie out of one eye while she came back in, pulling at the pins under her arms, and the silk threaded off in a long trail on the floor while four arms and four legs reached up, swaying, to pull her down, and began to wrap around her. The kaleidoscope was somewhere under somebody now, lost in the maze, and I squinted and everything was gone but the center of the scene, and there I saw an opening like the brown rubber lid on the Lepage's Mucilage, winking, oozing, winking. The person from Michigan held up a card from the game that said *Kiss your partner like you really mean it*, and I was aware only that he held his lips on mine past the delicate point when it's no longer a kiss but something else—a rest, maybe. We had rolled so close to the fire that my clothes smelled as if someone were ironing, and I kept my eyes closed in case, against all odds, Aunt Ruth had brought her ironing board in and was actually trying to work during this party.

The person from Michigan and I made it through the game until past two o'clock, and I remember excusing myself while Maggie and one of her partners continued to throw the dice and kiss, throw the dice and drink, throw the dice and I went back to the bathroom—it's a game of stamina, of testing your mettle—you're on your honor not to give up and I could hear them endlessly throwing the dice and laughing, and throwing the dice, and I dropped onto Debbie's bed; they threw the dice and he was in the bed on top of me and I could smell that he had thrown up, too, and I heard the dice rattle and I tried to pass out but couldn't.

And then we were silent in the darkened room, while the music from the party moved in intricate patterns all around the edges of the bed. I closed my eyes hard and I could see a purple design in the dark, feel a cold silken smoothness sliding between my legs, cold, smooth, and I could taste the dark wine he breathed into the air. That was all.

When he was gone I opened my eyes to see the damage, and I saw I was covered with moonlight on the bed. It was streaming in through Debbie's window, through her eyelet canopy, a shower of light coming down on me in tiny droplets. I pulled my arm up from the shadows and it was webbed with luminescent lace, and my stretch marks made a silver hammock of my soft belly. When the wind blew the tree branches outside, the patterns in the room shifted so that gray pearls of light were flung against the ceiling. They embroidered the walls, the bureau, and fizzed like champagne bubbles across the mirror and through the windows until they hardened into pointed stars outside in the night sky. I thought they must be coming from me when I took a breath because I felt as if I were floating under water . . . the whole bed was floating . . . Drop by drop by drop the little bubbles rose when I breathed, freezing like crystal beads on the dark web of intrigue I had hung from the corners of the room. Drop by drop by drop, and I fell deeper until the weeping-willow branches were floating above me in the cool watery darkness outside like thick seaweed. I was alone, a dark creature floating in the center of lights like a black widow on a web of dew.

I woke. Over at the lace curtains on the window I clearly saw my pearl necklace flashing there, miraculously all back together again, and then I felt Aunt Ruth putting it on my neck again, and suddenly she ripped them apart and threw them at me again and I was sleeping in my bed in her house again with my bureau pushed against the door to keep her out. But she came in through the window, her dark eyes flashing like burning coals, and she played with the broken beads as if they were marbles, or dice. She rattled them in her fist and threw them against the wall, and they were snake eyes, and she wasn't afraid of them. She arranged them in a pretty design on the floor and grew a tree of life that dripped spangles and sequins. She put some in her pocket for the quilt and tied a piece of the broken string around my finger so I would never forget. She was writhing, dying in an orgy of pain, and I would never forget, never, never, when her fingernail tore through my palm as I held her hand.

I looked down at my hand. I wouldn't forget. But there was only my wedding ring and the grinning gargoyle scar on it. There was no string. Was I dreaming? To try and remember? The beads were still flashing in the lace at the window, and I was afraid to get out of the bed, afraid they were all over the floor . . . the beads glowing like snake eyes, a mummy's eyeball in the dark, and I knew that if I lifted my head from the pillow, one would shine at me from the corner like a cat's eye in a car's headlight. I fell asleep again, I think, seeing the beads in my old tiger trash can, in my saddle shoes, under the bed, and still flashing, flashing, at the dark window, glittering lights in my dark tea, in her black coffee.

Suddenly a sword of light slashed the room in two, and then a white frame appeared on the wall as someone slowly opened the door. She pushed her head into the room and the brittle voices of the strangers from the party blew in, scattering the dreamy white pearls and gray bubbles.

"Are you all right in there, Linda?" she whispered into my black void.

My voice moved thickly through the dark air to answer the light at the door. But it was too weak to break through the surface tension that surrounded the brightness, separating the dark from the light.

"Can you come out? I've got a big problem," she whispered. It was Maggie. It was always Maggie.

She closed the door, pulling the swirling darkness after her like water down a drain, and the room was full of black dreams again. I waited in the darkness, gathering strength, and then I moved from the bed.

I turned the clown's nose on the light switch, and Debbie's room appeared again, the room of my pastel gingham daytime dreams. There was a Winnie the Pooh bag holding her sneakers, and Holly Hobbie on the sheets, Barbie and Ken in their A-frame ski lodge, and my pile of clothes on the floor. As I bent to find my underwear, I felt a slivery wetness slither down my leg and I realized that yes, it had all really happened. Under water. There were lots of dead fireflies on the floor beside my halter top, under Debbie's eyelet curtain. I sat at her dressing table and looked in the Snow White mirror at the dark circles under my eyes and at the whiteness of my cheeks, and I couldn't decide if I looked like the Wicked Witch yet, although I certainly wasn't Snow White any more. I brushed my hair with her brush, which was shaped like Cinderella's slipper, and some peanut shells fell out, crinkling onto her jewelry box, and I wondered if she believed in all these fairy tales as much as I still do. On the wall, Gretel followed Hansel into a little chalet, where the time, 4:35, was surrounded by painted bluebirds. Before I left the room I smoothed out the quilt I had made for her before I really knew what I wanted her to know about me, and now there was a pale-yellow stain from the person from Michigan across two of the plaid babushka squares. I turned out the light and went to find Maggie.

The living room looked like a war zone—empty of people now, but full of their debris. It was a Pompeiian scene of petrified despair crawling toward the doorway at me. It seemed that a stone had been thrown into the calm surface of my life, and now everything yellow I used to think about when I stood in this room was swirling around the stone and disappearing.

I went outside to look for Maggie. But first I sat down on my front lawn to try to let my head clear. The tree branches were flung like black threads against the gray sky, all knotted together. Maybe nothing was making any sense any more, because I was looking at the whole thing from the wrong side—maybe the knotted branches are really fine embroidered net, seen from the clouds, beautiful if you look down at it, scrambled if you look up. Or maybe the pattern in things is in the spaces between, not the branches themselves. In what is not said in the night, rather than what *is* said. Or maybe the pattern only shows up when the wind blows, and the real pattern is the movement, the dance . . . or maybe there is no pattern at all. I was completely on my own—nothing could help. I got up to go find Maggie.

She was standing out back in my driveway, next to her car, which must have just fallen out of the tree it stood under, it was so smashed up. The fender was crumpled back on itself, as painful-looking as a bent-back fingernail, and a long savage splinter zigzagged through the wooden frame from the fender. Maggie was leaning against it crying, while the moonlight glittered off the silver maze that a rock had made of the windshield.

Now the retribution from the sin starts, I thought, but Maggie was crying with anger, not remorse. "Goddamn sonofabitchin creep . . . bastard! He can't let me have anything . . . he has to ruin everything . . . he fucks his brains out with the nurses, but not me, never me, and I go out for one night and have a few laughs, get a little high, and he wrecks the one thing that's really mine in the world . . . I can't have anything around him . . . he hates me! He hates me!" She was shaking the little car with her hard sobs and I don't think she was talking to me, but she kept on talking, crying, "He says I emasculate him . . . He's forcing me to leave . . ." when suddenly she stopped. "Oh, my God," she screamed, and then she was running down the street even before I could try to stop her, which I wouldn't have necessarily done, because I was hoping her crying would lead her away from Chuck and Open Marriage, and in her hysteria maybe she'd tell if she'd slept with Jack, and then I'd be off the hook—I wouldn't have to feel so bad about tonight. But she was gone, running, screaming, "If he hurts it, I'll kill him, I'll kill him!" And I thought for a moment that she might be worried about Amanda, but then I remembered the piano and realized that I would have to go down there myself now and gather up Debbie and Toby before all hell broke loose.

That's the one big problem with being a mother. Even with semen from a man who is not your husband dripping down your leg and a raging headache that makes you feel as if you could tear up the lawn in fistfuls with your bare hands, you still have to go and get the kids. And they will still be so sweet-smelling and innocent, totally protected from you and your messy life, as they sleep on your shoulder.

It was now starting to get light, bringing the day that would bring Jack back, as I walked past the darkened houses that separated my house from Maggie's.

I listened for raised voices. This much commotion surely couldn't go unnoticed, but there was nothing. Maybe this really is a Potemkin village and the reason nothing makes sense to me is that I'm on the wrong side of the flats. The houses slept on as I walked past, all was safe behind the little beady Automatic Failproof Burglar Alarm Protection buzzers and dots of light. Maggie's house was still completely dark and I got in through the back porch, past the giant sleeping mattress pad with Maggie's gray cat sleeping on top, and found the kids in their Superhero bags in the game room, safe and unaware of the night. Toby was cold, curled up tightly, like a bug when you touch it. His cheek under his sucker blanket was as warm as a fresh miniature waffle, all woven with the thermal pattern, and his pajama tops were unsnapped, showing a pink ribbon of skin. Little boys in spacesuits were rocketing across his chest to a little yellow moon, and over his diaper a cowboy with fringes flying was roping a calf. I picked him up and tapped Debbie to wake her. She was frowning and curling in on herself on the couch, her nightgown wrapped tightly around her long legs. Roses were strewn all over her delicate back. I leaned over and shook her, and I could smell her breath. She was in foreign countries again. I woke her and quietly left the house, with Chuck and Maggie somewhere deep inside, their voices picking at each other like twigs crackling in an unseen fire. Only Harvey Wallbanger's yellow almond eyes watched us as we went out, and down the dark and silent neighborhood street.

The refrigerator motor cycled on again, and a puff of cold air, dusted through with baking soda, blew against my face, scattering the dark scents of last night. I stood up, pushed the vegetable bin back into the refrigerator and closed it. It was now perfectly clean. Of course, I also considered not telling Jack anything at all, but I was more afraid of making the orgy invisible, of filling the ever-growing space between us with an insane circus of bodies that only I could see. So I went in to clean the living room, but I felt like a dog with my face being pressed into the mess I had made. The sun beamed in like a policeman's searchlight, routing the images of the night before, sparkling off the trail of Maggie's silver straight pins in the carpet. It was so hot that the room still smelled like strangers and the ashtrays were glutted with red pistachio fingernails and fat dusty elbow macaronis of cigarette butts. ESS IS ESS— I could spell out Maggie's magic saying from her wall collage with the cigarettes. She said it had mystic significance because new letters could be added so it would read either "Bless This Mess" or "Cleanliness is next to Godliness": it was the essence of this senseless mess. I decided to leave it all a little longer and get back into bed to repair myself with a tiny nap before Jack got home. The house was more resilient than I—it could wait an hour.

But when I lay down on Jack's side of our bed, Debbie's bed kept floating back up. Although I wanted to think hard about why exactly I had thought it was going to be such a good idea to go to bed with a complete stranger, the picture I needed floated away each time I grabbed at it, like the good witch in the bubble when Dorothy lands in Oz. I knew I had some sort of feeling for the person from Michigan, but it was nothing more, really, than I feel when I pull into someone's driveway just to turn around. I knew I desperately wanted to have an orgasm, because I had the idea that when you do, it's like making an oily spot on a piece of parchment paper, and for a second your body, which is the paper, becomes transparent and you can see through to yourself. But since I prefer there be a pane of glass between me and my emotions, so that I can see what's hitting it rather than feel anything directly, it's just as well I didn't have any orgasms . . . or I'd lose my Winky Dink screen.

The oily spot is like the spots on the grease-dotted hoagies Aunt Ruth used to make and wrap up at the sandwich store where she worked. I sometimes came downstairs to watch her as she worked at the counter. She was bitter, matter-of-fact, and she always seemed to be mad at me. She would slap a long, hard roll on the speckled Formica and then slice it, from the side, spinning the roll under her broad, sharp knife. Crumbs would fly from the crust as she pressed the splayed roll down and then gouged out some of the bread from the center of it. It all happened so fast. She splashed olive oil onto the roll from a ginger-ale bottle with a sprinkler attached to the top, the same kind of bottle she used to dampen clothes with when she was home. Then she spread fingerfuls of onions, tomatoes, and red peppers over the oil-soaked bread. She always had peppers under her nails when she came home, and I was always afraid she wasn't coming home.

My chin was level with the counter and I watched in terror that she'd be hurt as she sliced meat and cheese at the big white porcelain meat machine. The round blade spun with a loud whine and caught pieces of prosciutto, boiled ham, and provolone as her fingers pressed the heel of the luncheon loaf closer and closer to the blade. The circles of meat would fly from the blade into her wide palm, and machine-like, her arm would swing over to the roll, and she would lay the slices of meat one by one over the other. The scallops of meat would advance and cover the tomatoes, the onions, and the peppers, slowly filling the sandwich, and then she would turn the machine off. It always stopped with an angry snarl, as if disappointed. She always said that the machine wanted to take a bite out of her, just like everything else in this world. Then she threw the pearls at me. And, finally, I remembered they were supposed to have been hers for the day she got married, and now she was giving them to me, since she knew she was never going to use them. Now. Why now?

She wrapped the sandwiches tightly, snugly, like little babies swaddled in giant sheets of heavy white paper that had transparent spatters of grease on them. She put the sandwich on one corner of the paper and then quickly rolled it up, tucking in the ends and sealing them with white tape. She labeled them with a crayon, and then the people came and took them away. She always smelled like onions to me. I wished she were around now to wrap me up the way she did those sandwiches. And then I remembered the cancer, embroidering along in its invisible pathways, the most insidious of all the invisible things that can hurt you. I felt I had to move very slowly through that memory, through all those colors and images.

I remember the wind that particular day—the wind eating at my skin as I walked home from school with my science project, which had gotten the best grade in the class. It was in the bottom half of a cardboard beer carton, and the wind was trying to balloon under the dish towel she had given me to cover it up with, puffing itself into the box with my project, so that it looked just like I was carrying home a roast turkey in a carton instead of my sand scene of Egypt. The last turkey I carried home, from the Catholic Charities Appeal at our school, got thrown out into the trash, unwrapped, before I could even explain that I never asked for it—they had just given it to me. When I got home this time, I went into the empty kitchen and waited for her to come in. I shut the wind outside and set the box on the kitchen table, and looked all through the house for her—in the bedroom, the basement—but she was gone. I got some milk and started setting the scrambled Tootsie Roll palm trees and cardboard pyramids back into their places in the sand, hung the Q-tip scroll back on the camel's saddle. She had written something in Russian characters on the brown-bag papyrus—that touch alone probably won me the prize, although her favorite pieces were her cottonball lambs, which still smelled like the aspirin bottle with their little glued-on rottini tails. I waited, and the shadows from the pyramids tilted and lengthened slowly like dark syrup across the sand, and still, still, she didn't come home.

Now I lay frozen under the quilt, feeling like a church window that someone had covered with blankets and pounded with a mallet. If you peeled the quilt away, you'd find another quilt underneath, and that would be me, glittering in this empty sunlight with all these memories. I remember I watched Howdy Doody first, and then Winky Dink, and still she didn't come. When the news came on, I could taste electricity in my mouth, I was so afraid they were going to say they'd found her dead somewhere. It was nearly six o'clock, and so I went outside to see if she was coming down the street, maybe with groceries. The wind, waiting, blew the front door back at me, and pushed into the living room, rattling the silver fringe on the floor lamp, and tussled with the lace curtains at the side window. A round salmon-colored pillow blew off the couch and rolled across the floor.

I ran around to the back yard and nearly screamed in terror when I saw them there, madly thrashing in the wind like flags of surrender. The clothes—the laundry—it was all still on the line and it was nearly dark. The sheets were sailing high, high over the line, in ribbon undulations, and with a smart snap they pulled at their clothespin moorings. They spread wide and bluish in the cold twilight, miles over my head, a semaphor message I was afraid to interpret. I grabbed at the clothes prop that held the lines, but it scraped out of my hand and rocked back and forth against the wind like a devil's metronome, giant and relentless, ticking away the black hours.

I kept still and covered up and quiet, and a car came swishing down the street below my window, all the way from 1953, and behind my eyelids I saw the white Venetian shadows rise up to the ceiling. I picked the splinters from the clothes prop out of my hand and watched through the window as the clothes, out at last at night, danced up to meet the first raindrops that came with the dark. I turned on the kitchen light and went back to the window to watch for her. I saw my own face there; deserted, with raindrops tracing past the black craters that were my eyes. And then I heard a car door slam and I knew she was coming home. I knew the bad thing was going to happen again. Then there was pounding on the back door, pounding, and I rose up out of the memory and got out of the bed, because I also knew it was only a matter of time until Maggie came.

She was still banging when I got to the door to unlock it.

"Boy, do you look terrible!" she said. "I thought an active sex life was supposed to put roses in your cheeks at least." While she talked, she took off a fuzzy beige sweater that she was wearing in this incredible heat and folded it carefully. She dipped into the living room and picked up a piece of the cheese that must have gotten shoved under a table, sniffed it, and threw it into an ashtray, knocking over a candle that had burned a black hole into the center of an apple. She looked at the torn quilt I had thrown over myself to answer the door.

"In general, I'd say you're falling apart," she said, walking into the kitchen and then stopping to poke her finger through a spider's web in the kitchen window frame before she sat down at the table. "Messy, messy! Very messy . . . this place is beginning to look good!"

I leaned against the sink as I filled the teapot and wished she would leave. I'd seen a week's worth of her last night. Her wrecked car was gone from my driveway, and she seemed to have forgotten that she was here almost all last night. Suddenly, now that it was clean-up time, it was my orgy, not hers. She was sitting in a direct path of the sun at the table, and to look at her was painful, because her hair shone as if it were on fire, and it was floating in delicate strands all around her head, as though she'd just broken through a spider's web herself. I looked at the just-washed floor and wondered if she would notice it, instead of all the mess. She interpreted my downward look and slump against the sink as signs of misery and dejection, and so she started talking again, suddenly inspired.

"Well, how's it feel to be an official adulteress? Are you going to tell Jack?"

"Do you want some tea?" I asked. She usually refused because she could never decide if she would stay long enough to finish it when she did come over, but this morning it looked as if she was feeling sorry for me, so she said, "Thanks, half a mug."

I turned from Maggie and tried to look into the past one more time.

I knew Aunt Ruth had gotten dressed up to go out that day because her black work shoes were in the closet and her patent-leather purse was missing. I looked through her closet, and my favorite dress, the red-and-white polka-dotted one with the big flat buttons, was gone. The tub was wet and the soap was soft. The lid was off her jar of Mum, and I smelled it and rubbed some on the back of my hand so I could think she was nearby while I waited, hiding in her closet. Hiding. "I'm sorry there are no lemons," I told Maggie from the sink. "I threw them out when I cleaned out the refrigerator this morning." I sat down across from her and pulled the quilt down around my legs and took my first sip of tea. My corner was in shadows.

"So you've been cleaning the refrigerator. You're already on a little guilt trip?"

"Why not? I'm enjoying the guilt more than I actually enjoyed the sex. And it's given me lots of new things to think about."

"Like?"

"Like how sick my aunt was when I thought she was just a mean old lady."

Maggie's eyes narrowed and glazed when she realized that I was serious. Remember, I told you that people never want to hear what you have to say.

"You mean the one who made that quilt? *I'll* say she was

sick! She'd have to be to make that, right? So, she was a sick old mean old lady. So what else is new?"

Maggie is the only person I've ever met who really believes in the Smiley-face poster that says, "Today is the first day of the rest of your life." That yesterday gets burned away by the morning sun. That nothing matters but her.

I watched the sun on her flowered blouse as it changed the colors in it from red to gold to rust, and then back to gold again as she breathed. The little hairs on her fingers looked fuzzy in the bright light.

"So, are you going to tell Jack?" she asked again, squeezing the tea bag against her spoon. She took a long swallow while the tea was still scalding hot, steaming in the air under her nose. I always wondered how she did that.

"I don't know, I haven't even begun to think about it yet," I lied. "First I've got to worry about getting rid of the rest of the actual party garbage, and then I'll worry about the stuff you can't see."

"Did I wake you just now?"

"Yes," I lied again. "Too much wine." I've been lying an awful lot these days—doesn't that mean there's something drastically wrong with your life if you have to keep lying and lying? If your car keeps veering to the left, you should probably get the steering wheel fixed, rather than give in to the pull.

"Thank God for wine," she said. "I wouldn't be able to stand Chuck without it."

"Well, we're beginning to sound like a couple of alcoholics, aren't we?" I said, because I thought a tiny touch of honesty, like a dash of bitters, might sharpen things up a little. Maggie got up to go. Too much, too soon—I can't seem to get the art of conversation down just right. It should feel like preventive dentistry, not the Spanish Inquisition.

"I never thought I'd say it, but I'm glad I married Chuck," she said, picking up her sweater. "He may not be exactly perfect, but he understands me, and he'll still be there when I come back if I need him. I could never stand being alone as much as you have to, but then, I'm not as strong as you."

I watched from my corner as, one by one, she turned the leather buttons into their holes until her shiny golden silk blouse was folded like wings into her woolly shell. I took another sip of tea, deliberately not moving, and said, "What are you going to do about your car?"

Maggie, pinned in a shaft of sunlight, stood poised while the question floated around her like bitter ether. She sniffed, and then turned her head. "I don't know, maybe I'll sell it or something. Chuck wants another Mercedes, and I know it's just going to sit there and rot in the driveway the way it's all ruined now. Neither of us will make a move to fix it because that would be like admitting feelings we're pretending we don't have for each other any more."

"But won't you lose your investment?"

"Maybe." She was playing with a button, turning and turning it in her fingers until it came off. I knew she'd never sew it back on, either, but instead throw the sweater away. "I'm getting tired of just letting everything go all the time, you know?" she said. She looked at me from deep away somewhere, and her voice was empty, the way your fingers are empty when you feel around and there's nothing and you're sure there was one more Raisinet in the box in the darkened movie theater, but they're all gone.

"What am I going to do?" She leaned her head against my doorway and her hair flattened out against the woodwork like a halo. "I just can't keep running away, giving everything up, just because we fight every now and then. He's the best thing I ever had. Yet I can't stay here either—it's such a mess . . ." She breathed out little dust motes into the air that spun away into the stream of light where she stood, and then vanished when they came into the shadows where I sat.

"Listen, why don't you help me clean up the living room, and maybe you can talk about it," I said.

She lifted her head off the wall and the halo shrank away.

"Sure, why not—I've done worse things. God, this place is really a mess," she said, lifting up her skirts and picking past the Passout game. "That was some party. I'm still sore . . ." And she eased herself into the fireplace chair, where she sat down on a long, grinning crust from the pizza. She put her feet up on the coffee table, and for the first time since I'd moved to the neighborhood, someone finally looked comfortable in my living room. I took the quilt from around my shoulders and looked at my watch: Jack would be home in about four hours.

"I don't have much time, do I?" she asked. "Ladybug, ladybug, fly away home. Your house is on fire, your children are gone."

"No, it's not that. I'm just trying to see how much time I have to get rid of all of this." I started folding up the quilt.

"You can never fold anything eight times, did you know that?" she said, and I knew she'd never watched Aunt Ruth fold sheets.

"See a pin, pick it up, all the day you'll have good luck," I answered, picking up some of her straight pins. "Did you know that?"

"Stop bobbing up and down—you're giving me a headache. Listen, sit down for a second, we've got to talk—all this can wait . . . please don't pull the clean-freak business on me again."

She could sense it, I knew. Crazy thoughts were racing through me to my fingers, making them twitch. If I could just wad up some of this cheese and get it into the fireplace, I could get to the three glasses on the mantel before she noticed. Then I could carry them and an ashtray back to the kitchen on the pretext of getting more tea. I had only four hours until Jack would be expecting his dinner.

"Can I get you something else to drink?" I asked, balancing, nearly crouching, on the edge of the carpet. One word from her and I could move, leap, undistracted, into the abyss of mindless work, of grateful straightening up, up, a clean sweep of movement through this slow, cadaverous drag of time. I waited while she looked at me. The word:

"Yes."

It's begun—I can move.

"Are you serious? I'm scandalized! After all you had last night—that you can even think of drinking! I love it! God, kid, you really are shaping up—here—reach me over the bottle . . . wait, no need to work—we can use these glasses right here—I mean, why go to any more trouble?"

And like a trapeze artist who just misses the bar, I'm falling down, down, into the humiliating net of this sloppy mess again.

"Ah! I can see that pained look on your face—you want to get something picked up, don't you? I'll help . . . What's this?" And she held up something small. "Look! It's a tiny little star earring, isn't that cute—not mine—not yours—it's pierced. Probably belongs to that fruity fat girl who thought she was a guitar. Tacky, tacky . . . Ach! My poor head, when I bend; my poor ass, when I sit . . . I got so twisted around last night, I felt like I was posing for Picasso . . . Listen, what I wanted to say is just this . . ."

And I sat down.

"You've got to understand that sometimes when people do things and it seems to affect you directly, they're not actually doing anything to you; maliciously, I mean. And besides, it's better not to believe literal things people say about people, words, gossip. Don't even believe what they say themselves. Words are so short of the real meanings people have. Are you with me so far?"

"So what are you telling me I should believe, then?"

"It's like the Bible, which is verbal, and God, who isn't. Believe in your gut instinct. Whatever your original feeling is about a person, you might as well go with it. I sound defeated, don't I?"

"Well, tell me what you're getting at."

"Our guts are not as self-serving as our brains are. I mean, if your stomach turns, that's natural, but your brain can really screw you up, wreck your whole body, and for no good reason. Of my rations and my emotions, I'll take my emotions any day. Which is why I came to say goodbye, rather than just splitting, as would be the wise thing to do."

"You're leaving?"

"Well, obviously I'm not staying. All the violence I seem to bring out in Chuck—somebody's gonna get hurt one of these days if I stay—me or the kids, and I'm getting out. I seem to bring out the worst in people, and I can't figure out why, since I try so hard to be a positive force in this here particular cosmos." She took a long glub, glub, glub of the Mateus, and the place where her Adam's apple would have been throbbed. "Well, I'd love to stay and help you clean up, but I'm sure you don't need any more of my help. You know, sometimes I think they've got it all backward with the brain controlling the body—I'll bet you it's more like the brain's just sitting there, it's a dumb lookout at the top of a submarine or something, calling out the orders that are really coming from below. The body thinks! Only faster, better—it sends the hormones that make the brain get off its ass and move its legs and even if you don't want to go, you go."

And then she got up, and the chair held her shape in its lap for a long minute afterward and then breathed out. The crust from the pizza was gone, either absorbed into the chair or clinging with its ragged tooth marks to one of the folds of one of the layers of her skirt.

"Can I take the rest of this wine with me? It's gonna be a long drive."

"You're leaving right now, this minute?"

"Oh, yeah, I almost forgot, I set it all up for you so Sherry will call you one of these days for tennis—don't waste your time with some of the deadbeats around here, like that idiot who sits around in her greenhouse all day. There's nothing wrong with you. Sherry will take care of you if you're straight with her, but stay away from her Aaron, or she'll claw your eyes out and then eat them in front of you. Aaron doesn't go in for the stupid games Chuck gets off on—you'll be out of your league there. He's a real ramrod."

"But wait, Maggie, there's something I've got to know about . . ."

She turned full blast toward me, and the tiny black wedge in her eye glinted, and when I saw her eyes flash, I thought that if she had been sleeping with Jack, maybe I'd just as soon not know. "Oh, yeah! it was the gypsies—whatever did the gypsies do to their kids?"

She thought for a minute, and then another, and another, and I'm sure Jack's plane was by that moment descending, coming in to land, breaking through the very clouds above our heads. Finally, she brightened, as the old story glinted off her memory. "Of course! Jack and the brace business! Now I remember. You are an unbelievable nitpicker, or you don't forget a damn thing. They used to put them in pots, and when the kids grew up and broke out, they were still shaped like pots."

"Oh, God—"

"It's not that awful, really. Look at it this way: the kids were artists! And besides, they made their parents a fortune at the circus. See ya around . . ." And she leaned over and quickly kissed me on the cheek. "Take care . . ." And she was already out the door, with the light tangled in her hair, caught at the moment of blazing, like the trees in the fall, those reds and golds, the colors in the fire, the setting, the separating sun. The pizza crust swung back and forth as she walked away, hanging on for dear life.

It took me only about an hour to clean up the living room, and while I did, I felt as if I were clinging to a secure rock while something was washing the less secure, like Maggie, away. Maybe I'm going to end up like Lady Macbeth, washing and washing and washing what will never come clean. Or maybe Maggie is like the miner's canary, the one that is the first to die if the air's no good. Maybe there's something wrong with this neighborhood and the rest of us are too dense to sense it yet. But if you look out the window, nothing has changed. And once the room is cleaned up, nothing has changed here either.

I checked the time and listened for Toby to wake up from his nap. He was still sleeping off the interruptions from last night, and Debbie was back balancing on her head outside, waiting for me to push her over. I've got to get out of this house. The orgy was fine while it lasted, but the minute it disappeared into time, the minute I cleaned it up and it was over, invisible, it entered the world of the ghosts, and now the ghosts are in an uproar over it. If I stay in here, I'm going to have to make them an offering, and I'm afraid of what they're going to want this time. This time I'm afraid, really afraid.

Something has shifted with them, I can feel it. Aunt Ruth is angry—she wasn't in the kitchen holding out a piece of toast for me when I came in just now, with little specks of black crumbs in the yellow margarine because the toaster is on the blink and she's late for work. Nothing. Somehow I think they think I'm one of them now that I've actually gone through with it, and now they're not going to take care of me and hold my hand and scare me any more. Now they think I'm one of them. Richard Speck has left my closet and is waiting to shake my hand. I saw Charles Manson put his bloody knife down for a second to applaud quietly when I took the chickens out for dinner. Aunt Ruth will hand me her sewing needle and say: "You mend the rip for me now, won't you?" If I stay here.

At least I haven't contaminated the outside. I found Debbie on the front lawn, where it slopes down to the mailbox, and I decided to stop being so honest with her about life. A little lie here, there, and at least she'll have the confidence to somersault. So I sat down with her and told her about the power of positive thinking, of the imaginative hope that can help a person to leap over physical barriers, stand immense pain at the Olympics, conquer space and time. The Winky Dink sort of thing—you get the screen and you'll be happy. Then I put her in proper somersault position and told her to think of success, to think only of rolling, of completing the motion successfully.

"Picture yourself doing it, doing it, and you will, you'll be successful," I lied.

Then the bigger lie. I turned her body ever so slightly toward the sun and bent her head to the grass so that her positive thinking could take place at the top of a gentle but significant slope in the lawn, and God would take her the rest of the way if that's the way He wanted her to go. She felt her first somersault, and I went back into the house to cook the chickens. When I looked out the window a half hour later, she was still continuing with her chain of circles, her green knees were in the air, her brown hair was speckled with grass bits, and I heard her voice trailing behind her saying, "Turn, turn, turn."

There is, I should note, no slope on the side of the house, so she was doing it on her own. And there is no sunlight in my kitchen at that time of the day.

It's too bad, but the one thing Maggie couldn't allow herself was the time to let things accumulate naturally, the way Aunt Ruth could. Maggie always made a great, bursting try, and then after that, she had nothing. But there is something to the kind of thing that gets done by doing just a little every day: you save a penny a day, every day, lose a pound a week, every week; the Chinese were supposed to have driven you mad by dripping a single drop of water on your forehead, minute by minute by minute, until your skull looked like the Grand Canyon and you screamed, "I'll talk, I'll talk!" Water is the universal solvent, more powerful than acid or Coke. Drop by drop by drop can be a potent force. The reason Jack and I had to get married was because I didn't believe a shot glass of beer a minute could get anybody drunk.

When Jack finally came home that evening, I was determined to tell him, to clear the air of the ghosts, and to make a new start as a good person. When I heard his sports car pull up into the driveway and then stop with a rumble like an empty stomach, I started on my plan. I went to the sink and began chopping the onions for the salad, while the chickens bubbled in the oven. The onions were supposed to make me cry, so that I would be in tears when he walked in. I was taking no chances.

He came in and kissed the back of my head.

"Smells good," he said, as usual. "And what's in the oven?" And how's the trip, chop, chop, chop, the solitude, and no tears would come. Chop. Where's the mail, slice, chop . . . anything doing while I was gone? . . . nothing. Absolutely nothing. I picked up the dead center of the onion and sniffed it. No smell. Was I going mad?

"What are you doing?"

And then I remembered—of course—Hints from Heloise: if

you keep the onions in the refrigerator, they won't make you cry. Carmen Miranda was a cold, cold lady under all that fruit.

I looked up at Jack, who was looking with great longing in the oven window at the two chickens roasting there. Behind the spattered glass you couldn't smell them and he couldn't know how close to going bad they were, and so I did a brave thing. I went over to the oven, walked right between Jack and the chickens, and turned it off. The light flickered and the oven blacked out. "I've got something to tell you," I told him.

He looked at me with such a look of innocence and surprise, and hunger, that I chickened out.

"I think the food is spoiled—we can't eat it. We're going to have to go out and get something. I can take the kids next door."

"God, Linda, I'm dog-tired! Can't you just make me a sandwich or something?" He opened the refrigerator and smelled the clean emptiness there. "Anything?"

"Everything's rotten—I had to throw it all out. There's nothing in the house— C'mon, we'll make it fast . . ."

He whimpered, but picked up his keys.

The gardening neighbor took a long time to answer my knock, and when she finally came, her hands were muddy and covered with a green moss.

"I've been playing," she said. "Just put the kids out in the greenhouse; I'll watch for you when you get back. Follow me," she said. And the kids did.

I've always felt that the gardener has the best chance for surviving and understanding life. She interacts with life, plays the game. My move, I plant; your move, it rains. My move, I weed; your move—killer frost.

Ten minutes later, Jack and I were blurring down the road at fifty miles an hour in his green sports car with the top down. He shifted into third gear and the car leaned around a curve; the colored lights spun past as he accelerated back into fourth. I was feeling lightheaded and giddy with danger.

"Do you want to get high?" I asked him. This was another thing we had learned from Chuck and Maggie.

"Did you bring anything with you?"

"Lots, lots . . ." and I reached into my pocket for the pipe and plastic bag.

"Sure, why not—the evening's already shot to hell," he said. "Hold it down so it doesn't blow all over."

Ah, it was good to have him home again so I could be told what to do. My hands were shaking as I tried to light it, and the flame from the lighter bounced and wavered and then went out.

"I think the lighter's empty; do you have any matches in here?" I reached for the glove compartment, naturally.

"Don't go in there!" He whipped his hand across, protecting it, before I could reach the handle.

"So what's in your glove compartment that I can't see?"

"Nothing, nothing, nothing. It's packed and everything will fall on the floor if you open it, that's all."

I didn't believe him.

"Here's a match," he said, reaching into his vest pocket, and he pushed his cigarette lighter in for extra insurance. I tried again to light it, and the match blew out from the constant wind vectoring over the speeding shell of the car. I could picture it curving over us, making an invisible shape like a 1950's Chevy around the boxy sports car. I knew this wind existed because once, on a bet, we had driven with the top down in a blinding rainstorm, and as long as we kept moving fast on the turnpike, we stayed perfectly dry, protected by the tapering envelope of the invisible rushing air. Only when we stopped, which was a stupid thing to do, did we get soaked. And we stopped because I couldn't believe in the wind and he finally had to prove it was there. I would never ask him to stop again, after that experience.

"You're really going to have to get down, there's quite a breeze tonight," he said. "God, am I tense! It's time to stop this rat race and slow up some."

I leaned far down in the bouncing car, into the darkness near the glove compartment, and thought I might throw up.

"Remember the time I threw up in your mother's car, her brand-new one, the second time we went out?"

"Just light the damn thing."

"Touchy, touchy. It's worth remembering." Because when you're married you're supposed to listen to what the other person wants to say even if you couldn't care less. That's part of the contract. I thought I would think about it a little after I got stoned, so I finally managed to light the pipe. I inhaled a little and passed it to Jack like a mystic offering. The little black hairs inside his long, straight nose were lit up for a second as he drew on the pipe, and I remembered the hairs on Maggie's fingers when she was drinking the hot tea. I keep putting the two of them together. He passed the pipe back to me, and I thought of silent ancient Indians from warring tribes passing a fragrant peace pipe to a person they might scalp in the morning. I inhaled deeply and felt my head clear, and my ears began to tingle with the night air blowing past.

I loved riding in the convertible. All the stars were racing by on the blackboard above our heads, and I thought of a song by Doris Day about using the stars as chalk to write something high above you. I tried to remember what those words were that got written up there, and also what I wanted to remember after I got stoned. The short-term memory loss was kicking in. Unfortunately, my long-term memory was quite intact, and I waited for an opening to tell Jack the truth, a moment when he would be ready and the wound wouldn't be fatal. I was going to tell him the truth, so help me God.

I only saw Jack at widely spaced intervals, when an approaching headlight would light up his face. Then he would disappear again. He *was* good-looking—Maggie was right. In fact, they belonged together like the "two most popular" in the yearbook who hated each other but got together anyway for proms and photos, just to make the rest of us feel bad. But he was mine—I owned him. Then, a headlight would flash past his face and he would disappear again. He was out of sight most of the time, and then I remembered the other things. The glove compartment—the throwing up. He didn't get upset at all; he just went into his mother's trunk, took out the shorts to his gymsuit, which he had worn that afternoon in tennis practice, and mopped up the vomit on the floor. He told me to sit back and not worry about a thing, he would take care of everything. And he has. The glove compartment. Maggie.

Maggie! Her very name is like a bell, routing the Indians, and the chalkboards, and even sweet Doris Day, throwing them out onto the sidewalk. By an immense act of will, I pushed and pushed a sixty-second breath of smoke into the deepest parts of my lungs, into all the branches, so that my lungs would expand and send it floating up into my brain and smother, obliterate Maggie. Go away, get out of our car! Begone! I started coughing, hacking, choking, and then laughing at the same time, because I pictured her as a little gnat being puffed out with the exhaled smoke, tumbling and rolling into the air. Or as a little spark of grass seed that explodes and then dies on the car's upholstery, red hair aflame.

"Are you okay, there, Oh, great smoker?" he asked. "You're a walking advertisement for what's going on in this car. Here, police, over here . . . this person. Come and get your pot smokers. We'll be put in jail, behind bars, for Christ's sake." He looked over, grinning. "Try to control yourself."

"Sorry." I was giggling now, and this was the first time today I had laughed, maybe the first time this week. I leaned over and turned on the radio, a simple, innocent act, and who would think that tumbling out of the car dashboard would come such incredible, tacky music—a thousand violins filling the car, moaning voicelessly, "Strangers in the night," to the fast black rustle of taffeta skirts swirling.

"Since when do you like that kind of stuff?" I asked his rather stony profile, a Mt. Rushmore of Pollution Control, blurring past the trees.

Unanswered, that question joined the ranks of the millions we had let pile up between us during the hundreds of hours of solitude while he flew around the country. Then there were more.

"Where are we going?"

"Why?"

"What are you thinking?"

"Are you feeling anything?"

"What?"

"What were you going to say?"

"Shall we do another pipe?"

"What do you mean by that?"

It never matters who's asking the questions. We would switch off: one of us would punch, the other would play rope-a-dope. And then, after that round, we started jabbing at the How to Improve Our Marriage theme, and to be safe, I offered up the knot I had tied myself: I-don't-like-myself-we-can't-have-sex-we-get-tense-you-don't-like-me . . . I could go on and on, but you get the general pattern. Only tonight, I was going to break the chain.

"In what way don't you like yourself?" he asked.

"In any way—the way I dress, the way I look . . ."

"What do you mean? The way you look is fine. Maggie said you look younger . . . damn." He winced, I think. I couldn't see clearly.

"I also don't like Maggie. Why do you keep bringing her up? Are you fooling around with her?"

"Of course I'm not fooling around with her—she's your best friend."

"She's no more my best friend than . . ." and I trailed off and kept the "than *I'm* my best friend" to myself.

"Do you *want* to fool around with her?"

"I *want* to fool around with everybody. You know that—you know how frustrated I am."

"I'm sorry. I think if my body hadn't gotten ruined, I wouldn't feel this way."

"It's not ruined, Linda. You know I love it, stretch marks

and all, and so would anybody else if you would just open up to people instead of being so covered up and cold."

And suddenly I panicked, because I was thinking he was getting too close. "I think there's a curse on us," I said, to throw him off by making him think I was crazy.

"What do you think this curse is?"

"It's lies, lies, lies. I lie to you and you lie to me. There's no truth at all between us. I fantasize about every man I see . . ."

"About Chuck?"

"Of course about Chuck, and Tom, and Dick, and Harry, whom you've never met." I had heard this conversation somewhere before.

Where . . . here . . . in my own house . . . in my own mind . . . those words stayed in, these words went out: "And I imagine that you're doing it with everyone you meet on the road, fooling around with the stewardesses, with half the women at work, with Maggie . . ."

"I am."

"What?"

"I am."

"When?"

"Whenever I get the chance."

"Where?"

"In hotel rooms, at work, at their places . . . in Debbie's bed . . ."

"In your own daughter's bed?"

"Here . . ."

"Here? In this lousy little car?"

"In this car, your car, her MG . . ." and he reached into the glove compartment and took out a package of rubbers. "I can prove it," I heard him say, throwing them in my lap.

"What does this prove? Why do you need rubbers? Doesn't she take the pill?"

"No."

"Why not . . . ?"

"Because, you idiot, Chuck can't get it up—they don't ever have sex—*you* know that, he's a wet noodle."

He pulled the car off the road and put his head down on the steering wheel, and I heard the crickets all saying, "Tsk, tsk, tsk," and I knew the salespitch was coming, and I thought, oh, my God, what have I done, because now he was starting to cry. Who knew he was a wet noodle? What a waste! Those shoulders, the teasing; what kind of person gets stood up by a wet noodle? Had I now gone beyond frigid?

Then he was crying on me, repentant, crying, telling me the truth, and I knew that there it was, there was his truth, he got his in first, all spread out so I could see it, be blinded by it. It was worse than my everyday reality of him, which I had learned to live with; worse, because now I couldn't feel any pity for him. Before, when my paranoia about his traveling and the secretaries had been especially bad and he did something nice to make me stop believing my bad hunches about him, I would feel incredible pity for the beating I put his reputation through. He would bring me sticky buns, and I would think him a sterling character, and he was, because he was always being polished by the gauzy embraces of my soft pity. It was all so dependable. I was the bad seed, he was the good egg. Instead, he really was a worm. A creep, a cheat. The dark waters of the lies had parted and I could see the seabed, and it was full of slime and corpses, mangled things. He was crying something about he was afraid I'd hate him . . . and, sure enough, there on a street very much like our own, with crickets singing and warm breezes sighing, I hated his guts.

I wanted details, of course. I probed him with my tongue the way I would probe a new cut. The more he cried, the more supple he became in my arms, the more I could bend him. I smoothed his mossy hair, stroked his curved spine, again and again, as he leaned into me, wrapping around me, and my arms encircled him until he was shivering and all rounded like a bow with his guilt. I sat straight beside him, tightly strung like a wire from his forehead to his hands, and he thought as he bent over me that he was playing on me, like a harp, drawing soft, forgiving music from my tense nerves with his plying fingers. But slowly I pulled back, slowly, slowly, bending him toward me until ping! And I flew away from him, finally freed from the pull of guilt. I blew away from him like a long, feathered sigh into the sky. I had used his confession to escape from him, and now my guilt was gone.—He was so sadly human; he was just like me.

I looked into his eyes and saw they were as vulnerable as waiting targets, black-centered, gray circles rimmed in red, and I turned away because I couldn't tell him my secret now. I knew to sting him that way would be the end of everything, and when I looked again, he was wiping his eyes and smiling, and we were saved for a time. The dark waters closed again, but we had both seen that incredible bottom of the pit for a second in each other's eyes. There was no more going back into the past now, so he turned the car around, right in the middle of the road, and we went home, while the silence darted back and forth between us like a devil's darning needle, mending the rip in our fragile black fabric of lies.

I put him to bed when we got home and told him that everything would be all right, as if he were my child; that we would talk about it in the morning. He cried a little more, and then I rocked him and he fell asleep, more peacefully, probably, than he had in a long time. I knew I was going to have to carry that orgy around now and keep it quiet, and so I rocked myself for a while, too.

When I went to pick up the kids, my gardening neighbor suggested they just sleep the rest of the night there, undisturbed, in the greenhouse. She handed me a bag of small dwarf apples, perfect and shiny, from her first harvest, and then she pulled something covered up with a sheet out of the greenhouse.

"Here—put this on your porch for me, would you? If it grows, you keep it. I'll carry it back for you." And she came home with me, dragging a giant potted begonia that was bigger than Toby's stroller, behind her on a wheeled platform. In the light I could see that the delicate pink petals had been rained into the brown dirt and that bugs had eaten the leaves into lace. And now that I've learned that I can eat the blossom of the day lily, it doesn't mean that I like it any less.

She picked off the browned leaves, using her thumbnail as a snippers, and held up one of the lacy ones. "Do you know that something even this far gone can be planted, and if it's cared for properly, it'll grow?"

Suddenly I was afraid I was going to cry. All the time I had just spent with Jack in the car while his tears wet right through my jacket and blouse, and I sat there without crying, and now I thought, I'm going to cry over a little chewed-up leaf. I never cry.

"I'm sorry, Mrs. . . ."

"Flossie—just call me Flossie! No need to be distant now

that the Tomato Blight has left the neighborhood. If you get my meaning . . ."

"Did you know about Maggie leaving?"

"Who doesn't? Good news travels fast around here. Her neighbors from down the end of the street want to join hands and dance around that house now that it's going to be sold. Maybe we could all form a bucket brigade and get the place scrubbed before it goes on the market. What a waste! But! Life goes on—just water this and I think it'll get through the wintertime. The fur on my oak tree is light, and I think we're going to have an easy dose this winter—but don't forget the water!"

"I'm sorry," I began again. "I wasn't listening closely. Do you want this plant back if it grows?"

"Poor child! Of course you feel bad! The host always feels a little weak when the parasite is pulled off. She was sucking you dry—everyone could see that. You're lucky to be rid of those people before they did you any real harm—we all are. Why don't you just go to bed? You look exhausted."

"Everyone could see?"

"What do you think you are on this corner? Invisible? The walls have ears, you know. By the way, did you ever have any luck with my baby tears?"

This conversation was becoming unreal. "Baby tears? You have a baby? I didn't know you had a baby . . ."

"No! No! No! Baby tears—the plant! The little plant I brought over last fall—did it ever grow in your west exposure out there on the porch?"

Of course! It was still where Amanda had thrown it, on the porch, behind the milk box. Dead as a doornail, too, I figured.

"I'll check on it sometime," I promised.

"Why not look now, while I'm here—there's no time like the present." While she picked around the begonia some more, I went out and got it. I pushed the box aside and there, in the wedge-shaped space between the wall and the box, was a pillowy triangle of green stems and tiny leaves. It was growing out of the pot on all sides—green threads were crowding out the hole in the bottom, and I had to break it away from the back of the milk box where it was growing, nourished all that time in the dark by the milky water that seeped out of the bottom of the container.

When she saw it, Flossie screamed in joy: "This is *marvelous!* It's wonderful! Well, *you* must keep it, because it certainly seems to love conditions here. But, for God's sake, let's get it transplanted. Do you have any good dirt?"

"Good dirt?"

"Good dirt—good rotting compost?"

"Well, I have lots of rotting things around here, but I never particularly thought of them as any good."

"Let me go get some and bring it over," she said, putting the browned begonia petals in her apron pocket.

"Well. Okay then, I'll see you tomorrow?" I said as I closed and locked the screen door after she left. She walked across the twelve or so sidewalk squares from my house to her house in quick little steps, and turned and waved. I counted as she went in and out of the light from the street lamp. The plant clung in gentle silk threads around my hand as I watched her go. Ten-eleven-twelve, one-two-three, change partners, and dance. Now it was my turn. I waved back, before going inside.

I had one last job to do before this day ended and that was to mend the quilt. I carefully pulled it off the bed, and Jack hardly moved, except to curl tighter around my cold pillow, waiting for me. His breathing was congested now from crying, and little squeaking sounds were scraping hard from his nose as his chest rose and fell. He was singing the real music of the spheres, as the celestial onion skins sadly scrape by one another and our layered universe spins toward the dawn. I rolled him over on his side so he'd be less stuffy by morning, and pulled the rocking chair over to the window. I turned on the floor lamp and watched and waited for Jack to come home from work again so we could do this evening over again, so he could make everything turn out all right. The hidden sensor had tipped the street lamps on, and now they stretched ahead like a long, hopeful rosary into the night. Every time I rocked in this chair, I waited for Jack to come home, and now, finally, here he was, home for good. I knew it—he was going to love me—he had to, now.

I took up the quilt. Watching and waiting, watching and waiting, the rocking forces you to pick up the cadence of the rocking of the cradle and the rhythm of the tides. Everything is beautiful . . . falling down, picking up . . .

I will have to work along the same exact stitches that Aunt Ruth drew if I'm to fix her quilt at all. It will mean that I have to pick up the pattern of her stitches, to feel her hand on top of mine.

I hear that car pull up again, and I hear her get out again. She's still crying. Her face is pale, her red lipstick is all chewed off, and I watch in the deep darkness from her closet as she climbs on her bed and hugs her patent-leather purse, and it is 1953 again, and when she finally falls asleep, I will creep out of the closet and go back to my own bedroom. She is very sick, and now we both know it.

"All those years? Why didn't you tell me?" I shout to her across the spaces of time, as I stitch.

"What could you do about it?"

"Why did you go on for twenty lousy years with your insides rotting and never say a word to me?" I ask the quilt.

"What would be the point of telling you?" she breathed back through the fabric.

"So I could have helped you," I beg her to hear.

She had cleaned up most of the mess she'd made from her tantrum before she went back to bed, I suppose. I'd never really know, so it all could have been a dream, all the noise and commotion as I pretended to sleep in my bed, except for my scene of Egypt. It was missing from the kitchen table in the morning, and there was sand crunching under my saddle shoes all over the kitchen floor when I got my breakfast, and there was a Tootsie Roll palm tree outside, in the shadow of the clothes prop.

And I knew that Maggie had called Jack at the motel during the orgy last night, because the Laughing Cow cheese had made a grease mark in the yellow pages next to the phone number of the Holiday Inn where he was staying. When I took the cheese out for Toby this morning, I could see the transparent triangle there, right on top of Jack's number, so I knew, but didn't want to look too closely. I wanted to be told, like a child, by either Jack or Maggie, that it was all a bad dream—everything was going to be fine.

And I really could have pretended that there was nothing wrong with Aunt Ruth that night and that nothing really happened, except when I left for school, she was still in bed, asleep in her dress on top of the bedspread, and the red dots on her collar moved lightly with her breath against the white sheets. I covered her up, and when I got home from school, the clothes were picked and folded away, and she had already begun to cover it up herself, so we never brought up the cancer again, while I lived there.

And when I went into the kitchen for more beer for the person from Michigan, Maggie blushed and turned away from me against the angel, cradling the phone against her hand, and when I grabbed the kaleidoscope, of course I knew she had called Jack after hanging up on Chuck. I could sense the storm was coming and I knew that nothing would ever be the same again—that something was horribly wrong. Jacques Brel was sick and dying the whole time they said he was alive and well, but still we sing, we sing.

I took out a stack of Aunt Ruth's old index-card days and bent them so I could flip through them, making a movie out of the memories, and then, yes, I could see now what I couldn't see day by day: Aunt Ruth was running down, disintegrating, falling apart right before my eyes, while I begged for an Easter hat with hard cherries on it, or a prom dress with embroidered roses, or her pearls to wear with my wedding gown. And she gave me everything but the chance to be close to her. She locked herself away in her own pain, and I stayed outside, wind-whipped, and now I could do the same thing to Jack, if I wanted to.

How could I never have seen what was happening right before my eyes? Is there a mesmerizing motion that exactly mimics the motion of the earth, hypnotizing us into thinking we're not moving? If I pump the spinning top, there they are, Jack and Maggie, moving together again and kissing, moving together and kissing, while Chuck and I tip and nod our heads, tip and nod, letting them, ignoring them, pretending we don't see them. Is the earth spinning so fast that we think it's still? Or is God so big He's invisible? Or moving so fast we think He doesn't exist?

I opened the quilt and spread it across my lap. It darkened any room it was in, like Aunt Ruth herself. She had finished it in the last months before she died, sitting silently in her dingy house and sewing until it got dark, until her eyes burned. She cannibalized every dress in her closet, cutting embroideries from evening gowns, lace from bridesmaids' dresses, flowers from housedresses. She cut odd shapes and fit them together into whirls and spirals and then embroidered all around the pieces, over and through the silks, the velvets, the cottons. Since she'd gotten fat, most of the clothes she had left were dark—burgundy wines, midnight blues, olive greens. And now I knew she'd meant the quilt for me, and me alone—to tell me not to waste so much time, the way she did. "Don't do what I do—do what I say," she always said. And I think I know now what she was trying to say to me.

I looked at the quilt from another angle. It seemed to quicken as my eyes got tired. All the shapes with black in them began to form a pattern, like the lead frame of a stained-glass window, and I could see myself standing with Jack in the dappled flow of the altar light after the ceremony, while she watched, smiling, from the shadows. The red lines of embroidery throbbed like a network of veins, or a labyrinth, or the turnpikes on a road map. I could see Maggie's little red car driving up and down the neighborhood, back and forth, from one bright square to another. I squinted and thought I saw a small brown bug in one corner, and all the green shapes began to move faintly, like leaves, or dollar bills, or the squares on a felt game board. I felt trapped in the center of a quivering net, fighting again with Aunt Ruth, because we never had any money. Of course she couldn't get any help; she had to keep quiet and keep on working, so we could eat.

When I closed my eyes, I could feel the patches move closer, and when I opened them, they moved away again. Just like the rocking chair, in the shadows, in the light, dark, light, day, night, day, night . . . I feel as if I'm on a giant seesaw and on the other end is God. You're up, alive one day, and then plunged down, gone into the night. Sliding backward on the white ice, down into the cold snow. God is a game player and life is a puzzle, and He has the last piece, so we just have to wait until the end to see the finished picture.

Holy Mary, Mother of God, return with us now to those thrilling days of yesteryear, and now, rising out of the trees on the mirror of dark glass that I rock in front of, I see the full moon of my own face, and what money we did have sent me to the dentist. I have perfect teeth, white in the lamplight, straight and long, and when I dip back, I am gone. And then when I rock forward, I'm back again, with the stars on my face like so many startling thoughts. I was the one who kissed William Wharton while we all stood in line for confession, just to be mean, because he was the smartest kid in the class and I was the second smartest as long as he was there. I confessed it ten minutes later, but I can still see his red face, and the boys hated him more for crying than they ever did for wearing the brown corduroy pants, and I almost did the same thing to Chuck.

If I tell Jack all about the orgy . . .

"Will you ever learn?" she breathed. "Keep your mouth shut. Embroider. Lie."

But if I tell Jack, maybe he'll understand. Maybe he'll hug me and my skin will feel transparent and my soul will show through . . .

Aunt Ruth said nothing. I think I had her on that one.

I start sewing again.

"It's worth a try," she whispers, so faintly I can hardly hear her. The weeping-willow tree is blowing outside the window, tossing its hair in fits, the way she did when I put her head on the pillow.

I pull the thread up, up into the light, and then plunge it into the dark cloth, leaving a new rose behind. My arm is a metronome, a counterpoint to my rocking, keeping time, time, time, in a sort of chronic rhythm. Crosspatch, draw the latch, sit by the fire and spin. Take a cup and drink it up, and call your neighbors in.

"I knew someday you'd know," she says, when I've finished.

I gather up the mended quilt, turn off the light, because the dawn is coloring the window screen now around the edges, with the glowing sparkle, with the finest of silver threads, lighting up. I climb into bed beside Jack, cover both of us up with the quilt, and he turns and curls around me. I bury my face into his shoulder, into the fabric, where I can smell them both—Aunt Ruth's patches and Jack's dreams. I feel a wetness near my fingers and I think I must have pricked my finger on the needle, but there is no blood, only tears.

And then I'm finally crying, crying out the glass splinters and silver needles of real tears, rinsing off the window inside; crying because it hurts, and because she has finally come home.